EZIO FERRARI
FAMILY OF CROWS

Contents

DEDICATED TO ALL OF MY FRIENDS WHO
CONTINUE TO SUPPORT ME.
THANK YOU.

CHAPTER ONE
BERNARDO MORETTI

Ezio didn't like field trips. They were always boring, always awkward, and most times had nothing to do with what they were learning in school. Most kids liked them because they got out of class, but Ezio didn't care about that. The field trips were sometimes as boring as the classes themselves.

Today's field trip was to the Bank of Rome. *The most exciting place in all of Italy*, he thought to himself as he walked behind his group. Apparently, the Bank of Rome had something to do with their social studies class, but that didn't make sense. They were learning about World War II, not economics.

Ezio also hated field trips because he was never in a group with his friends. This time, he was in a group with three guys who were at the International Academy of Italy on athletic scholarships. One of them was in danger of getting kicked out because his grades were so low, and the other two put just enough effort into their schoolwork to keep their grades at passing level. Ezio didn't know them very well and rarely talked to any of them. He walked a few steps behind, knowing his place in their little group. He was going to get ignored until it came time to fill out their answer sheets, then all of a sudden Ezio would be their best friend just so he would help them with the assignment. It happened every time.

As the line of freshmen and teachers made its way down the street, they passed dozens of alleys. As they passed one alley, Ezio noticed an old man standing in the shadows. He was paranoid nowadays, but with good reason—anyone standing in the shadows could be an assassin. The Hône Order of Assassins would be coming after him in a little less than a year—maybe they got impatient and wanted to force him into the Order sooner.

Ezio had his guard up as they passed the alley. The old man did nothing; he barely looked at the high school students as they passed. Ezio relaxed slightly and allowed himself to breathe. Maybe his paranoia was getting out of control...

He quickly dismissed his thought when he saw the old man standing in the next alley. *How did he get there so quickly? Why is he there? Is he following us?* This time, the man made eye contact with Ezio.

"Can I help you?" Ezio asked, not at all considering that the man could be a perfectly innocent civilian. None of the kids in front of him heard him speak to the old man. For a moment, the man said nothing. Ezio slowed down, waiting for him to respond but ready to run if he needed to. The man nodded slightly.

"Follow me," he said.

Ezio had been taught at a very young age not to talk to strangers. But then again, he had kind of thrown all rules out the window when he and his friends went off to find his great uncle Angelo, who was an assassin. They ran off, spent hundreds of dollars on train tickets and food, and lied to their parents about their whereabouts. Ezio glanced over at his class, then back at the old man, who was hobbling down the alley. *What do I have to lose?* He darted into the alley and followed a few feet behind the weak-looking figure.

The alley was long and stretched on for five blocks. Several other alleys, most of them designed in a zig-zagging pattern, branched off from the one they were in now. At the end of their alley was a large field with brown, dying grass. They were at the top of a small hill, overlooking the suburbs. Ezio lived in what was considered downtown Rome—just a few streets away from the Trevi Fountain, the Bank of Rome, and the Colosseum. A small hut sat precariously at the edge of the hill, sagging a bit on the side where the land began to slope down.

The hut looked like it had been hastily built with wooden boards, a thatched roof, and a crooked door. Crumbling stone steps led up to the door, which hung loosely on its hinges. The old man hobbled painfully up the steps and opened the decrepit door. Ezio peered inside and saw it was dimly lit by a single window built into one wall. The man lit an oil lamp, something Ezio had never seen in person before, and walked over to a cabinet.

"Watch your step," he muttered.

Ezio hesitated. The man didn't look like an assassin, but then again, neither did anyone else. That was the whole point: to never be suspected of being an assassin. But the man seemed too old, appearing to be much older than Angelo, and moved extremely slow. Ezio walked up the steps and into the dank little hut.

It took a moment for his eyes to adjust in the shadowy, musty hut. When they did, he saw there was a small wooden table with handcrafted chairs. There was a sink and a gas stove against one wall, and against the other was a small cot and a dresser. Against the far wall was the cabinet the old man was fiddling around with.

"Sit down," he said. Ezio pulled out a chair and sat. He watched as the man shut the cabinet door, turned around, and sat down across from him.

"My name is Bernardo Moretti. I wish to help you."

"Help me? How?"

"I was a part of the Order," Bernardo said with a sigh, unhappy at how his time had been spent. "I know all about them. With my help, you may be able to stop them."

"Wait, how do you know who I am?" Ezio asked. He had been surprised to find over the summer that a rogue NSA operative named Gabriel knew who he was, but then again, it was the NSA. They seemed to know everything. Were the assassins keeping tabs on him too?

"Every assassin in Italy has heard of the legendary Ezio Ferrari," Bernardo said, almost sarcastically. "You are next in line."

"Next in line for what?"

"Control,"

"Of?"

"The Hône Order of Assassins,"

CHAPTER TWO
THE MOST POWERFUL ASSASSIN

"What do you know about the Hône Order?" Bernardo asked. His voice was gruff and raspy, and Ezio wondered if at one time in the old man's life he had been a smoker.

"That they're going to try to make me an assassin when I turn sixteen. And that my great uncle Angelo worked for them." Bernardo nodded.

"They don't have to wait until you're sixteen," he rasped. "But I'll get to that in a moment. We should start at the beginning."

Bernardo got up from his seat and hobbled over to the sink. He filled a glass with water, sat back down, and got comfortable again. Ezio realized the man moved extremely slow for an assassin. *He must be retired.*

"In 1100, there was a man named Aetos. He moved from Athens to Rome when he was twenty years old, and from there he made his way up north. And when I say up north, I mean really up north."

"Hône," Ezio said. He already knew where the Order had been founded.

"The towns in Aosta Valley were secluded—the perfect place to form a secret society of killers. Forget

6

that it was cold and near the French border; that actually worked out for Aetos. You see, all of his assassins were not only trained to kill, but also to hide, to disguise themselves if necessary. That's where France comes into play."

Something clicked in Ezio's head. Over the summer, before he and his friends had left Rome to find Angelo Lombardi, they had found a note hidden in his grandmother's living room. The note had been written in French, for reasons unknown to Ezio at the time. But now it made sense.

"All the assassins are fluent in French?" he asked.

"*Oui*," Bernardo replied. "The newer, younger, assassins aren't as fluent—if they even know how to speak French at all—but that's not my point. My point is, Hône was the best place for Aetos to form the Order. No one ever thought to look there. Some people didn't even know Hône existed." Bernardo paused to cough, furthering Ezio's suspicion of him being a smoker.

"Aetos' plan wasn't to kill people just for the hell of it. He had the corrupt politicians and political enemies of Italy killed. The Hône Order of Assassins was a godsend for Italy in 1100. It was Aëtius who ruined it all." Bernardo took a sip of water before continuing again.

"Aetos wanted the leaders of the Hône Order to be his descendants. His son, his grandson, his great-grandson—you get the point. They were all named Aetos up until 1170. Then they changed it to something a little more Roman: Aëtius. Because of Aëtius I, the Order's headquarters were moved from Hône down to Rome, but they kept the castle in Hône as a training facility. Aëtius was obnoxious and arrogant; he didn't believe in the same things Aetos had. He screwed up the Order, had his assassins kill people he had personal issues with. He used his rank as an assassin to intimidate officials into giving him government jobs. He was as corrupt as the people Aetos had once killed."

"Did Aëtius get killed by his assassins?" Ezio asked. Bernardo laughed, as if the idea was preposterous.

"No. Of course not. The assassins loved Aëtius and began killing their own personal enemies. But then it all went to their heads and they started killing people who looked at them sideways, and then that evolved into killing random people on the street. This went on for over a hundred years, and the Roman army began hunting the assassins. There was a war—a war no one knows about—between the Hône Order and the Roman army."

"Why doesn't anyone know about the war?"

"Because the Romans are too proud to admit they were defeated by a group of 2000 men. Italy would be the laughing stock of the entire world."

"Did the army do anything to try to stop the Order?" Ezio asked. It didn't make sense that a country could let murderers run rampant.

"No, but they didn't have to. The war was in 1295, and lasted only a short while until the assassins got bored. A little over twenty years later, the leader of the Hône Order was Aëtius VI. He didn't like the way things were going with the Order, so he decided he would change it a little. And with those changes came his son, Ezio I."

"Let me guess, I'm Ezio 9000?" the boy asked sarcastically. He had caught on to the naming pattern. Bernardo smirked.

"You're the twenty-seventh Ezio since 1316," the old man replied. "The current leader of the Hône Order is Honorable Ezio XXVI."

"Honorable?" Assassins didn't seem like very honorable people.

"He's not a descendant of Aetos I. He is the temporary replacement of Angelo Lombardi, who is Ezio XXV. You are Angelo's real replacement."

"But I don't want to be his replacement. I don't want to be an assassin." Ezio said earnestly, and Bernardo nodded in understanding.

"I know. That's why I wanted to talk to you. I think I figured out a way for you to get out of this."

"Really? How?" Ezio sat up straight in his chair, excited at the thought of stopping the Order.

"You go after the leader of the Order, a man called *Arcangelo Della Morte*,"

"Archangel of Death," Ezio translated, the name sending a chill up his spine. Bernardo nodded in approval.

"Angelo trained him years ago, before you were born. Arcangelo lives in Hône, as all leaders of the Order do, in the castle Aetos had built as the training center back in 1100. He visits Rome one week out of every month to make sure everything is running smoothly down here. But for the most part, he just hides out in Hône."

"I take it you don't like Arcangelo?" Ezio asked. Bernardo didn't seem very fond of the leader.

"Not particularly," he said with a slight grin. "The man's crazy. Which brings us back to my first point: Arcangelo doesn't have to wait until you're sixteen."

"He doesn't?"

"No. Not at all. The typical age for initiation into the Order is sixteen, but anyone can be trained earlier if they're good enough. Angelo was trained his entire life by his uncle, Ezio Renato Lombardi. You know Renato as your great grandfather's twin brother. Maybe the prolonged training is why Angelo was such a legendary assassin." There was a significant change in Bernardo's tone compared to when he was talking about Arcangelo. It was as though at one time, he and Angelo had been friends.

"Did you know Angelo?" he asked. Bernardo nodded.

"We worked on a few missions together. He's a good man." Ezio scoffed. *Good man? He wants me to become an assassin. He's a killer. How can he be good?* Then he remembered: *Bernardo's a killer, too. That's why Angelo's a good man. They're the same.*

"You may think your uncle's a criminal, and you're right," Bernardo said, seeming to read Ezio's mind.

"He was a criminal, and a downright cruel one. But when you meet Arcangelo, you'll swear Angelo

Lombardi is a saint." *I doubt that*, Ezio thought, but he said nothing.

"Arcangelo could snatch you off the streets anytime he wants. But he won't because of the pact between your father and Angelo. Assassins are men of their word. But if Arcangelo really wanted to, he could train you today, or when you're seventeen, or when you're forty. But he will train you, no matter what. You are the one they've been waiting for."

"What do you mean, 'the one they've been waiting for?'" Ezio asked. Bernardo was making this sound like he was a part of a prophecy or something.

"You're the legendary Ezio. The one that will bring the Hône Order of Assassins back to greatness. Nothing that Aëtius VI did could ever make the Order the empire it had been prior to the war. Nothing Ezio I ever did could compare. No one could bring the Order back to what it was. That is, until now." Bernardo paused again to cough. He coughed violently this time, a wheezing, loud cough that racked the old man's body. He drank some more water and cleared his throat, pretending as if nothing happened. His voice was weaker this time, and more serious.

"There was an assassin. He was young and hopeful, like a doe. Poor fellow thought the Order would be the greatest organization on the planet. He was a sort of historian for the Order, and he believed that one day there would be a leader, much younger than any of the others, who would unveil the Order when Italy was least expecting it. It's been hundreds of years since the government's known about them. Well, I guess that's not true. The majority of the government has no idea the Hône Order still exists. There are a few people that Angelo and Arcangelo have paid off. The corrupt officials know about them."

"Do any other countries know about the Order?" Ezio asked. Bernardo nodded.

"The United States, Mexico, Great Britain, Colombia, Syria—but again, only certain people in the government know. I think China knew back during World War II, but I'm pretty sure Renato made it seem to them as though the Order crumbled after the war."

"So if all of these countries are aware, even if not everyone in the governments know, how come nothing has been done to stop the assassins?"

"Greed. It might not seem it, but the Hône Order is a lucrative organization. It makes it's money off of hits, extortion deals, briberies...you get the point. The politicians who know about the assassins are a part of all that. They are the ones who order the hits. They are the biggest criminals of them all. Corruption, personal greed...it drives these politicians to keep such a dark secret."

Ezio processed this. He had known corruption existed in practically every government out there; it was inevitable with all the power and money that came with political positions. But what he hadn't known was that governments could keep a murderous society like the Hône Order up and running. During Ezio's lapse in questioning, Bernardo continued bombarding him with information.

"You are supposed to be the next leader, but just because you hold that position doesn't mean you hold the power. Undoubtedly Arcangelo would be the mastermind behind all of your orders and endeavors; your name would just be assigned to everything. Arcangelo's plan is to expose the corruption in governments to loosen citizen support, incite riots, and, when the governments are at their weakest, take over. Primarily, take over Italy. From there, the Order may be able to take over the rest of Europe." Now the Hône Order was just sounding delusional. It sounded like they were planning world domination. It was childish, and almost comical. But Ezio knew it was a very real threat, especially if the Order got a hold of him.

He tried to imagine living in an occupied country. One occupied by assassins, who made up a relatively small yet ruthless group. Life would change drastically, and the world would never be the same. Not with the Order in charge.

"Arcangelo has to know that there's no way I would ever help him," Ezio said, the idea of aiding the assassins in any way completely blowing his mind.

"Of course Arcangelo knows that. But do you think he cares?" Bernardo snapped. "He's crazy! Whether you help him or not, the fact that he has you under his thumb will be enough to scare Italy into giving up. Your reputation precedes you. You're made out to have supernatural powers."

"But I don't. Super powers don't exist. Don't people know that?"

"Maybe they do, maybe they don't. My point is, the fact that you're alive and still bound to your father's pact is enough for Arcangelo to act on. Your name is what makes you powerful. And because of that, Arcangelo won't settle unless you're an assassin or dead."

"I have no other options?"

"You could kill Arcangelo," Ezio stared blankly at the old man, hoping he would laugh or tell him he was kidding. But Bernardo did neither of those things; he only stared back at Ezio with the same expression.

"You're not serious, are you? I mean, can't I just leave the country or—" Deep down, though, he knew there were no other options.

"You can leave the country, go into witness protection, do whatever you want. See what happens on your sixteenth birthday. The best case scenario is you'll be taken, uninjured, to Hône or one of the other training facilities. The worst case scenario is your family will be killed and you'll be trained in a jungle somewhere." Bernardo's bluntness angered Ezio. Wasn't he supposed to be helping him? He wasn't doing a very good job of it.

"So my only options are to kill Arcangelo, die, or become an assassin?" Bernardo nodded. Ezio leaned back in his seat. "There's got to be some other way—"

"If there was don't you think I'd tell you?" Bernardo asked, pounding the table with his fist. He was angry too. Angry that he couldn't help the teen escape his fate. "Look. I hate this as much as you do. Maybe not for the same reasons, but I hate it. I hate

Arcangelo. I never wanted to become an assassin but because of him, I did. Now look at me. There are only three ways to get out of this. You don't seem very enthusiastic about any of them. But I know you don't want to become an assassin and dying is out of the question, so that just leaves killing Arcangelo."

"If I kill Arcangelo, I won't be any better than the assassins I'm trying to avoid!"

"Would you rather kill one man or kill thousands indirectly?" Bernardo raged. "If you don't stop Arcangelo, he will take over Italy. There will be another world war. Thousands of people will die because of you doing nothing. Killing Arcangelo won't compare to what will happen if he lives."

"What do you mean there will be a world war? How do you know that?"

"Because with you around, there will be a renewed hope in the Order. They'll go as crazy as they did when Aëtius I took over. It'll be as though hell froze over and the devil himself was seated at the top of the world. Arcangelo has supporters in other countries who are aware of his plan and are willing to help him. They will cause chaos in their own countries, making them weaker so the Hône Order can conquer them more easily. But there *are* people who are trying to stop Arcangelo and the ensuing war. There are only four, though. Used to be seven, till two died and the third chickened out."

"Are they assassins?" Bernardo nodded.

"Assassins ready to give up everything just for your sake."

"Are you one of them?" Ezio asked. The old man nodded again.

"Not for much longer, though," he replied a bit sullenly. He gestured toward his lungs. "If Arcangelo doesn't get to me first, this will."

"Is Arcangelo going to kill you?"

"Probably. I mean, he's always wanted to. Now that he knows about the rebel group and who's involved, there is more of an imminent threat on my life. On all of the rebels' lives. We had our headquarters in Verona, but we scattered when Arcangelo first found out about us. More importantly, though, you need to be worried about the supporters of the Hône Order."

"Those are the people who will cause chaos in their own countries?" Ezio asked.

"Yes. Greece has a similar order in Athens. I don't know much about them but I do know they back Arcangelo in everything. When they found out you were supposedly the one the Hône Order's been waiting for, they started preparing for war. They're ready to help take down Italy, if the Order will help take down Greece."

"Great," Ezio muttered. He knew what had to be done, even though he didn't like the idea. "How do you suggest killing Arcangelo?"

In answer, Bernardo rose from his seat and walked over to the cabinet again. He removed a wooden box from one of the shelves and set it in front of Ezio. The boy lifted the top off and looked at the contents laid neatly inside. There were three knives inside, all different sizes. One was connected to what looked like a wrist brace.

"That is a hidden blade," Bernardo said, pointing towards the knife connected to the brace. He took it out of the box and slipped it over his wrist. "It'll be a little big on you, but it will stay hidden under a jacket or something." He removed the brace and put it back in the box. He replaced the cover and handed it to Ezio, who held it gingerly, ready to leave after asking one last question.

"So what do I do, just go up to him and stab him?" Bernardo shrugged.

"Stab him in the neck. It's most effective, and that's how all the assassins do it. It'll make it look like an inside job."

CHAPTER THREE
PALAZZO MADAMA

"You aren't really going to kill him, are you?"

"I don't see any other way out of this,"

"Can't you just talk it out? You know, take the high road or something?"

"I don't like it either, but I don't really have any other choice. I thought about it all night, and I couldn't think of any other solution."

Outside a coffee shop, standing on the bustling street corner, two tall, lanky, teenage boys spoke quietly about the Hône Order of Assassins. They were stalling; they were three minutes early for their appointment with a tour guide at the Palazzo Madama, a political building near their neighborhood.

It had been twenty-four hours since Ezio's encounter with Bernardo Moretti, which meant twenty-four hours since he had disappeared from the field trip to the Bank of Rome. Ezio's absence had gone unnoticed for only five minutes; then a manhunt began for the truant ninth grader. He had, inevitably, gotten a detention for "skipping" the field trip, although he had returned as soon as his conversation with Bernardo ended. But after his detention had ended, he and Santos Ogechi, one of Ezio's best friends from middle school, embarked on yet another school trip: this time to the senate building for a report.

"You always have a choice," said Santos a few moments later as he gazed across the street. "No one's bound by anything. Not what you think is your fate, not destiny, or whatever you want to call *this*." He emphasized *this* by waving his hand, as if the entire predicament was laid out before them on the pavement.

"But there's no other option that's presented itself," Ezio insisted. "Milan and I thought for hours yesterday. The only thing we've come up with is killing Arcangelo."

"Maybe it doesn't have to end that way," Santos said as a noisy crowd of university-aged students came out of the coffee shop.

"Maybe," Ezio replied.

"Want to head in?" Santos asked when the group had passed.

"Sure,"

Their tour was for a simple project given to them by their Italian teacher: go to their assigned historical building, take some pictures, learn about the history, and create a five-minute presentation on it. It was supposed to be easy.

The boys walked into the building and went through the not-so-attentive security checkpoint. They checked in at the front desk for their 3:30 appointment, then sat down on a bench.

The Palazzo Madama was a building that dated back to 1505. It had been built for the Medici family, and had once been home to the cousins Giovanni and Giulio. They became, respectively, Pope Leo X and Pope Clement VII. Long after the Medici family ended, the Palazzo Madama became the home of the *Senato del Regno*, or Senate of the Kingdom, in 1871. Now it housed the Senate of the Italian Republic.

Ezio, always observant, gazed around the lobby of the Palazzo Madama as he and Santos waited for a guide to take them on their tour. He noticed two men sitting on a bench near the elevators, and recognized one of them as Aurelio Conti, the President of the Senate. Ezio elbowed Santos and pointed Aurelio out to him. He was interested in the admirable politician for just a few moments before retreating back into his own thoughts.

Ezio kept watching the two men by the elevators. The man next to Aurelio wasn't a politician—at least, not one he recognized. He could have been a representative or secretary, or he could have just been a friend.

Something about the second man was off, though. Maybe it was the slight resemblance to Aurelio. Both men had long narrow faces and the same dark eyes beneath jet black hair. Aurelio looked a few years older than the man next to him, having a more worn out disposition about him. He was dressed in a navy blue checkered suit and brown shoes, and had a gold Rolex watch on his right wrist. The man next to him was dressed in all black save for a crisp white tie.

Ezio turned his attention away from the men and looked over at the glass doors. Every so often, one or two people would come in, going through security with barely a pause and heading straight for the elevators. Most of them acknowledged Aurelio with a nod of the head or a polite greeting as they waited. He stopped long enough to smile back at them before continuing to quietly talk with the man beside him.

Everyone that entered the Palazzo Madama looked similar: almost all of them were dressed in a suit or dress, and they each carried a briefcase or purse. They all seemed to be in a hurry, as if they were late for a very important meeting.

Ezio glanced at his phone and saw it was 3:36. The tour guide was late. He sighed inwardly and went back to watching the well-dressed businesspeople. Twenty seconds later, the doors opened again, and a man and a woman entered. The man paused and held the door for another person, and as he did so, his brow furrowed in judgement. Ezio soon realized why.

This newcomer was dressed in a brown suede jacket and jeans. He had long, curly, blonde hair, and the beginnings of some patchy whiskers. His clothes were wrinkled, as if he had just spent the day traveling. He was tall, with broad shoulders, and stuck out in the classy lobby like a sore thumb.

Ezio noticed that one hand was in his jacket—not in the pocket—and the other was by his side. There was a strange glint in his eyes—eyes that were locked on the man beside Aurelio. The one who wasn't any sort of official he recognized, and resembled the senator.

Ezio had heard about the assassinations of presidents and other officials, and had read how some of those murders could have been avoided had bystanders noticed warning signs. Ezio, curious, had researched those signs. And right now, this strange man was exhibiting two of those signs.

Aggressive gaze, hand hidden where a gun could easily be concealed—the man seemed suspicious. Ezio didn't hesitate. He stood up and moved towards him as he continued on his path towards Senator Conti. As he neared, the man withdrew his hand and in it was the black shadow of a Beretta. Ezio lunged forward and sprinted towards the suede jacket. The man heard his rushing footsteps and turned, saw the teen had discovered what he was up to, and reacted swiftly. He raised the gun and aimed it at Ezio's chest.

Suddenly, it was as if everything was moving in slow motion. Ezio pushed the gun away a split second before it went off. A loud crack echoed through the lobby of the Palazzo. The bullet sailed through the air, narrowly missing Ezio's left arm, lodging itself into the wide wooden frame of a portrait of the first President of the Senate, Gaspare Coller.

Ezio tackled the man in the jacket, and they landed on the ground with a thud. The gun was knocked out of his hand, sliding across the smooth granite tiles.

The man shoved Ezio off him, sending the boy flying into the wall between the elevator and Aurelio Conti. The wind was knocked out of him as his back and head slammed into the hard wall. He struggled to his feet despite wanting to just sit down for a few minutes. His head throbbed, and the room was spinning around him.

Security guards rushed over to secure the President of the Senate and arrest the man who they thought tried to attack him. The man punched two of the guards, though, and kicked another in the chest as he began to flee. Ezio started to chase after him, but a fourth guard put his arm out to stop him. The teen, corralled by the guard's beefy arm, watched helplessly as the mystery man ran off.

"*Sta bene?*" the guard asked. Ezio nodded dazedly and glanced over at Santos, who was standing a few feet away, his mouth hanging open in stunned silence. He turned his head as far as it would go to look at the elevators where Senator Conti and his companion had been sitting. Aurelio was still there, looking very shocked as he brushed security guards away from him. But the other man was nowhere to be found. *That's weird*, Ezio thought. He hadn't seen the man run past, so he must still be in the building. *Why would he leave?*

"Well," he finally muttered awkwardly, shaking free of the guard's grip and walking over to his friend. "That was fun. Come on, let's get out of here."

The guard only stared at him, not able to comprehend Ezio's English. Though he didn't understand it, he could understand his desire to leave the Palazzo Madama before the police showed up.

The guards posted themselves by the Palazzo's doors, forming a sort of barrier to keep the boys inside while they waited for a bilingual detective.

"I want to thank you," Aurelio Conti said, walking over to Ezio and Santos as they sat unhappily on the bench. The tour had been postponed; no one, not even their guide, was allowed in the lobby since it was now a crime scene. "You saved my life."

Ezio felt like telling Aurelio that it wasn't his life that had been in danger, but he restrained himself and smiled at the politician.

"No problem," he said. "I'm—"

The doors flew open, cutting Ezio off mid-sentence. In strolled a thin man with a pointed nose stuck in the air as if he owned the Palazzo Madama.

"Abate!" he barked. A pale, almost sickly looking, younger man scurried into the Palazzo and stood attentively before him. "Assess the crime scene." The subordinate officer nodded curtly and scampered off to talk with the security guards and to take pictures of the bullet hole in the antique picture frame.

His superior grinned arrogantly, as if he had not a care in the world. Never mind someone had just discharged a gun inside the senate building. He was just happy he was in charge.

"We have twenty-seven minutes before the *Arma dei Carabinieri* get here," he said in an almost singsongy voice. "Where are my witnesses?"

A guard pointed toward Ezio and Santos, and the police officer strolled over to them.

"*Ispettore Capo* Nero Lagorio," he greeted, flashing his state police badge and then quickly stuffing it back into his overcoat pocket. "Which one of you saved *Senatore* Conti's life?"

"I did," Ezio said, stepping forward. *Ispettore* Lagorio gave the teen a tight-lipped smile.

"Good. Your country thanks you. Now, do you mind telling me what happened?"

Ezio gave the detective his statement, as did Santos. But as he spoke with Lagorio, something nagged at him. *Your country thanks you.* That sentence ran through his mind a thousand times. *In less than a year, I could be the cause of Italy's downfall...and they're thanking me? Just wait...*

"Oh, one more thing," Lagorio said before turning to find the young officer he had walked in with.

"Probably the most important thing. What's your name?"

"Ezio Ferrari," he replied with a little hesitation. Something about the detective didn't sit right with him. He couldn't figure out what it was. It couldn't be that he was asking questions—he was a detective. That was his job. But something didn't feel right. *Maybe I just don't trust anyone*, Ezio thought. He had developed some minor trust issues over the past year, mostly because there were assassins crawling around with their sights set on him. To him, everyone was an assassin until proven otherwise.

"Ezio?" Lagorio articulated the name. "That's a fairly uncommon name, is it not?" Ezio nodded.

"You don't see it very often," he agreed.

"It's a historical name, too," the *Ispettore Capo* continued. "I believe there was an assassin named Ezio Renato Lombardi, back in the early 1990s. He was arrested three times, but never convicted of anything. He always had an answer for everything." A lump rose in Ezio's throat. Renato Lombardi? That was his great grandfather's twin brother. He had been an assassin? What did Lagorio know about the Hône Order?

"Did you work the case?" he asked, trying to keep his voice steady. Lagorio shook his head.

"No, I was much too young. But my superior," Lagorio said, wagging a finger. "He was very much involved in the case. His life's goal was to convict Lombardi. He was somewhat obsessed with the case. He told me all about it during my training as *Vice Ispettore*." Ezio was stunned. Renato Lombardi was Ezio's great-great uncle, which meant he was the one who trained Angelo. If Ezio remembered correctly, he had been five years old when Renato had died. That summer his father had traveled from their home in Chicago to Verona for the funeral.

Verona. A little lightbulb in Ezio's head went off. His eyes grew wide and he glanced at Lagorio with a look of sudden revelation.

"I have to go," the boy stammered. "I...I have soccer practice."

That last part was a lie, but Ezio didn't care. He grabbed Santos' arm and started dragging him out of the Palazzo, ignoring both his and Lagorio's protests. An officer tried to stop them, but Ezio barreled past him. He had to go talk to Bernardo.

Ezio jogged down the sidewalk to the alley he and Bernardo had used to get to the hut. He had ditched

Santos a couple blocks away when his friend refused to go any farther.

"Tell me what's going on," he had demanded. Ezio didn't stopped running.

"No time," he called, not looking back.

He dashed up the crumbling steps and pulled open the door. Bernardo was sitting at the table reading a newspaper, and he jumped up when the door opened. It slammed heavily behind the teen, rattling the small structure.

"Ezio? What are you doing here?"

"Renato was one of the rebels, wasn't he?" he said. Bernardo stared at him.

"Yes," he replied slowly. "How did you—"

"And Angelo's one of the rebels, too. That's the real reason why Angelo isn't the leader of the Order anymore. Arcangelo threatened him, didn't he? He threatened to tell all the other assassins if he didn't step down." Bernardo motioned for Ezio to sit at the table. He did so, waiting impatiently for his answer as a crosswind blew through an open window above the sink, ruffling the newspaper that now sat on the table.

"You're a smart kid," Bernardo said finally. "I didn't think you'd figure that out."

"Who are the other two people in your group?" Ezio asked.

"It's better if you didn't know. I'm not sure if Arcangelo himself knows."

"There was a guy who almost got killed less than an hour ago," Ezio said, wondering if he was connected at all. It couldn't have just been a coincidence. "He was sitting with Aurelio Conti on a bench at the Palazzo Madama. A man walked in with a gun and was going to shoot the guy next to Aurelio, and I stopped him. The police think he was aiming at Aurelio, because he's a politician, but he wasn't." Bernardo hesitated.

"Conti," he whispered. "What did the man with the gun look like?"

"He had blonde curly hair and was around six feet tall. He looked kind of like a surfer from California." Ezio worried the simile would be lost on the Italian native who had no TV in this little hut. But Bernardo seemed to understand perfectly. A strange look washed across his face, making Ezio anxious.

"I have to call Angelo," he said, scrambling out of his chair. "We're in danger—"

Suddenly, something flew through the open window, and Bernardo gasped. His face contorted in pain and bewilderment. His hand reached up to his neck, and he pulled out a small dagger. Blood rushed out of his neck at an alarming rate.

Bernardo made a sickening sound and fell forward, landing on the table in front of Ezio. Blood pooled next to his head, inching closer and closer to Ezio's hand.

Dazed, Ezio moved his hand away slowly, not able to take his eyes off the very dead man in front of him. His brain seemed to be drawing a blank, unable to comprehend what happened.

Something else flew through the window, but this time, it wasn't a dagger. It was a glass beer bottle with a burning rag stuck in the end of it. The glass shattered, the molotov cocktail exploding and setting the hut alight. Ezio was like a deer in headlights, watching in utmost terror as the fire began to rapidly spread in the dry wooden hut. He got out of his chair and started backing towards the door as the fire climbed the table and began engulfing the old man. The hut was quickly filling with smoke, the small window not able to ventilate it quick enough. He began to cough, and his eyes started to tear up.

He reached for the door and, to his horror, couldn't find the knob. He spun around and searched for it, fighting to look through the smoke. Sweating from heat and anxiety, he found the knob and turned it, and though it turned easily, the door didn't budge. It had gotten jammed when it slammed shut!

"You've got to be kidding me," Ezio muttered before a fit of coughing silenced his words. He needed to get out of here. He felt nauseous, and it wasn't just from smoke inhalation. He shouldered the door repeatedly, the oxygen deprivation beginning to get to him. Tears were involuntarily streaming down his face as he gave the door one last shove.

This time, the door gave way, and Ezio fell face first down the steps into the grass and dirt beneath the hut. He coughed a few more times and crawled forward, getting away from the burning structure.

His thoughts raced as he inched further and further away from the hut. Who had killed Bernardo? Why had they set the hut on fire? Did they know Ezio was in there with him? Was it the same guy from the Palazzo?

Ezio waited until his coughing subsided before climbing to his feet and stumbling into an alley. It was a bad idea to get up so fast, and the world around him began spinning. He doubled over and threw up where the pavement met the grass. The image of Bernardo's dead body and the blood pooled around him was engrained in Ezio's mind. He leaned against the wall, trying to get his breathing under control, and gathered himself. In the distance, he could hear sirens wailing, growing louder as they got closer. The emergency responders' reaction time wasn't too bad. *I wonder who called them.*

People on the streets looked at him strangely as he passed, but Ezio ignored them. He was more focused on getting home and avoiding his parents. He knew his face was probably blackened with ash, and that would cause his parents to ask questions. Questions he wouldn't be able to answer truthfully.

Chapter Four
New Leads

"So Angelo's really trying to help you? Why did he do all that stuff over the summer then?" Luke asked Ezio later that evening, his mouth full of *mozzarelline fritte*, or small fried mozzarella balls.

"I don't know. If I had to guess, it's because he wants me to become an assassin, but not in the sense like we were thinking. He probably wants me to be in the rebel group, like him."

"To help him take down Arcangelo,"

"Yes," Ezio replied. He had gotten home half an hour earlier, and had darted upstairs as soon as he walked through the door so he could change out of his darkened clothes and shower. He washed his face, scrubbing the ash off so no one would notice, and spent twenty minutes covering his hair in shampoo and running his hands through it until the water was no longer grey. Once he had gotten dressed and made sure there weren't anymore signs of the fire, he invited his friends over and told them what happened at Bernardo's when his parents weren't within earshot.

Ezio was sitting at the dining room table with Milan, Luke, Giovanni, and Santos. They were Ezio's best friends, and had been since he moved to Rome back in the fifth grade, nearly five years earlier.

Luke, Giovanni, and Santos were like brothers to Ezio, but Milan was now actually his brother. Foster brother, to be exact. In October of 2013, the Ferraris adopted Milan, who was an orphan and spent most of his summers at a boys' home in New York City. Not wanting him to be miserable any longer, the Ferraris welcomed him into their family. Maya and Tony treated Milan like a third son, and the other kids called him their brother when asked who he was. Milan was as much a part of the family as anyone else.

"Who do you think the guy with the gun was?" Giovanni asked. Santos shrugged.

"Probably some psycho who had it out for Aurelio Conti," he said. Ezio glanced up at his friends.

"He wasn't going to shoot Conti," he told them. His friends stopped eating their cheesy snack and stared at him.

"Who was he going to shoot then?" Milan asked.

"The guy next to him. I don't know who it was. He didn't look like any politician I've ever seen."

"Why didn't you tell *Ispettore* Lagorio?" Santos asked, appalled information about the crime had been withheld. Ezio shrugged.

"They're going to take investigating it way more seriously if they think someone tried to kill the President of the Senate."

"But—" The doorbell rang, keeping Santos from arguing anymore. Ezio heard his mother go to the door and open it, and looked up just in time to see her troubled face as she let the uninvited guest into the house.

Ezio stood up when he heard the deep whispery voice. He and his friends knew who it was. They watched as Ezio crossed the threshold into the living room, which led to the front hall.

"Ezio, this man is with the police. He wants to speak with you about what happened at the Palazzo." She seemed worried, hesitant to let the man speak with her son. Ezio grinned at her reassuringly.

"That's fine," he said. "Me and Santos can handle it." Maya gave her son a look, which he met confidently, and his mother reluctantly walked away. He had told her about his heroics at the Palazzo, and though she was proud he had stopped an attempted murder, she was also upset he had put himself in harm's way.

"What are you doing here?" Ezio hissed as soon as his mother had gone away.

Ezio had last seen Gabriel three weeks earlier, just before his fifteenth birthday. Ezio and Gabriel had met to discuss their next move—whether to track down the Order or just make a plan for his sixteenth birthday. "Maybe we should just kill them when they show up next year," Gabriel had suggested. Ezio had refused to use violence, but that was before he met Bernardo Moretti. Before he discovered his sixteenth birthday meant barely anything to Arcangelo, and that the only way to end this was to kill the leader of the Hône Order.

It was unusual to see Gabriel now, so soon after their last meeting. Ezio had figured he'd get a call from the rogue NSA operative in two weeks, and planned on turning him down because of all the final projects and papers he had to complete. The semester was almost over; he had three term papers to write and two projects to finish. One of those projects was the report on the Palazzo Madama.

When Gabriel and Ezio met, which was every five or six weeks, the meetings usually lasted no more than half an hour. There wasn't a lot to talk about—the Hône Order hadn't made any moves—so Gabriel often told Ezio about his time with the NSA. The two had come to trust each other more than they had over the summer. Gabriel trusted that Ezio wouldn't rat him out to the government, and Ezio trusted that Gabriel wasn't plotting against him.

"I think I found something," the middle-aged man said. "Is there somewhere we can talk?"

"Not till tomorrow. What did you find?" Gabriel's eyes flicked over to the others; out of the four boys sitting at the table, he had only met Milan. And that meeting only lasted sixty seconds, on a train.

"It's about the guy from the Palazzo Madama. The one you tackled?"

"How do you know about that?" Ezio asked, but regretted it almost instantly. Gabriel could find out anything he wanted. He was trained to do that.

"It was on the news," he said dismissively. It wasn't true; Ezio had seen the newscast and he hadn't been identified because of his age. "I checked out some security footage from the Palazzo and was able to ID the guy with the gun. He's a CIA agent named Tristan Clay. Well, soon-to-be *former* CIA agent. He's done at the end of the month. He's taking a last minute 'vacation' in Italy."

"Why was he at the Palazzo?"

"The man he tried to kill was Aurelio Conti's younger brother, Arcadia. And guess who Arcadia works for?"

"The Hône Order of Assassins," Ezio said quietly. Bernardo had muttered "Conti" shortly before he died. If Aurelio wasn't an assassin, then it had to be Arcadia. Gabriel nodded.

"The police are searching Interpol and the Italian databases. All the wrong places. I'm going to call them on Wednesday to let them know it's Tristan Clay."

"Why are you waiting?" Ezio asked.

"Because I think he's our guy. I think he's the guy Angelo had send me that false information about the hit on Sam. I think Angelo might have sent Tristan after Arcadia." Ezio shook his head.

"Change of plans, I guess. Angelo's on our side." Gabriel raised his eyebrows.

"How do you know?"

"I met an assassin yesterday. His name was Bernardo, and he told me that he, Angelo, and, I'm assuming, Arcadia were in this little rebel group that are trying to help me."

"Really?" Gabriel asked. He had always thought Angelo was the bad guy. He did seem like kind of a jerk, even when you looked past the whole murder-for-hire thing. "Well, if that's the case, then what's our plan?" Ezio glanced at his friends.

"We'll split up. You help Milan, Giovanni, and Luke find Tristan and figure out what he's doing here. Santos and I will go to Hône and deal with Arcangelo."

"Wait, why does Santos get to go to Hône?" Milan asked defensively. He didn't want to go kill an assassin, but he certainly didn't want Ezio to go do it on his own. He knew Santos wouldn't be much help—as loyal as their friend was, he wasn't about to murder someone. He had morals. So did Milan, but he was a little more flexible with how far and to whom those morals extended.

"Because Tristan's dangerous," Ezio replied. "And you know how to defend yourself better than Luke and Giovanni. You'll be like a bodyguard." Milan sized up his friends. Luke was short and had training in martial arts, but he wasn't prepared to use any of his experience in a combative situation. And though Giovanni was tall and had the build of a boxer, he had never thrown a punch in his life and his rather sensitive personality suggested he never would. As for Santos, his dad had been a real boxer many years ago, and he had taught Santos the basics of punching. He had some experience in defending himself. He would be alright against Arcangelo.

CHAPTER FIVE
TRACKING DOWN CLAY

"Mom, can Milan spend the night here?" Luke asked Laurie Russell the next morning as she sat at the kitchen table, on hold with her hairdresser.

"Sure, did you clean your room?" she asked. Luke grinned at her.

"Of course," he lied. "Thanks, mom!"

Milan followed Luke down the hall to his room, which was the furthest from clean he had ever seen it.

"You don't mind, right?" Luke asked about the mess as he picked up a couple t-shirts off the floor and threw them onto his desk chair.

"Nope," Milan replied. His room wasn't much better.

"Giovanni should be here soon. You want something to drink?" Milan was about to respond when Luke opened a door next to his bookcase.

"Whoa, you have a mini fridge?" Luke glanced up at him.

"Yeah," he said as if everyone had a mini fridge in their bedrooms these days. "Want a Coke?"

"Sure," Milan shrugged, and Luke tossed him a bottle.

A few minutes later, Milan, Luke, and his older sister Nicole were sitting around watching TV in the living room while the boys waited for Giovanni to arrive. A rerun of *Italia's Got Talent* was on, and one of the contestants was a man doing acrobats high above the stage.

"Wouldn't it be hilarious if he just totally face planted?" Luke said with a mischievous grin. Milan smirked and Nicole shook her head as she scowled; she thought her younger brother was immature.

She wasn't wrong—Luke knew he was immature and was proud of it—but he didn't understand why she got so annoyed with *his* antics. He was a carbon copy of their seventeen-year-old brother Logan, who called himself "the original jokester" of the Russell family, yet Nicole didn't have a problem with him. "Maybe two Logans are just too much for her to handle," Ezio had once said when Luke asked his opinion.

Logan and Luke could have been twins, had it not been for the large deficit in height. Logan stood at an average height for a boy of his age, while Luke lagged behind all of his classmates, clocking in at the third shortest in their grade. Their personalities were identical, as were their faces and hair—they looked a lot like their father, Ethan, who had the same dirty blonde hair and blue eyes.

Their two sisters, Nicole and Jaclyn, looked more like their mother. They all had straight brown hair and green eyes, which they rolled frequently. Nicole was eighteen and Jaclyn was twelve, and, unlike Logan and Luke, differed greatly in personality. Nicole was your typical teenaged girl—the kind who said "OMG" and "ugh!" way too much, who argued with her parents about going to parties and hanging out with friends late into the night, and who constantly had her cell phone in her hand. Jaclyn was the exact opposite. She was quiet and less dramatic, and she didn't have a cell phone yet to consume her time. She was close with Luke and actually found his jokes and pranks funny.

Nicole was rarely amused by Luke's immaturity, and today was no different. Luke decided to ignore her vexation and kept watching the acrobat, silently hoping he would face plant on the stage. Thirty seconds later, the act was over, and the man walked away without his face touching the floor. The host came back on the stage to introduce the next act, but just then, a light knock on the apartment door brought Luke's attention away from *Italia's Got Talent*.

"That's Giovanni," he said, getting up from his chair and walking over to the door.

"Just in time," Luke greeted his friend, taking Giovanni's sleeping bag and backpack and dropping them down near the door. "Sorry to rush you, but we've got to go to the Colosseum."

They were going to meet with Gabriel to discuss how to deal with Tristan Clay. It wasn't Luke's ideal way of spending a Saturday morning—he usually slept in until noon—but he wanted to help out.

"We'll be back in a little bit," Luke called to his mom, who was no longer on the phone. She waved to them as they filed out of the apartment, hurrying so they wouldn't be late.

*   *   *   *   *   *

"I set up the meeting for nine o'clock tonight, in St. Peter's Square," Gabriel told them, glancing around distrustfully. He was arguably more paranoid than Ezio, but that was because of his training. The NSA had trained Gabriel to be suspicious of everything.

"Vatican City?" Milan asked, wondering why an attempted murderer would agree to meet at a holy place like the Vatican.

"No, St. Peter's Square in Manchester. Yes, Vatican City!" Gabriel answered.

"The attitude's very uncalled for," Milan muttered. Gabriel ignored him.

"I'll be nearby in case anything goes wrong. Try to get as much information out of Clay before you call me in. I'll get the police and have him arrested."

"How sure are you that Tristan's the guy who gave you the false information?" Luke asked.

"Absolutely positive. Angelo admitted to falsifying the information about the hit on Sam. I got the information from a CIA agent, and no sane, loyal agent would ever just let information like that slide, fake or not. It was him."

"How did you even contact Tristan?" Giovanni asked next. "You said he's CIA. I thought those guys were really hard to find."

"They are. But their hotels aren't."

CHAPTER SIX
THE BEGINNING

While his foster brother and their friends were meeting with Gabriel, Ezio walked into the dining room, where Tony Ferrari was setting the table. Lunch wasn't for another few hours, but that didn't mean the plates and silverware couldn't be set up. Santos stood in the kitchen behind Ezio, unsure of what to do or say in this situation.

"Dad, do you remember what you said over the summer?" Ezio asked.

Tony froze. He remembered exactly what he said over the summer. In June, he had apologized for getting his son involved with the Hône Order of Assassins, and hadn't said a word about it for several weeks. But in late August, right before the start of the school year, Tony had talked about the Order with his son again.

"I still feel really bad," he had said. The two were stuck in traffic, heading home from a soccer camp Ezio had attended. "If you're going to deal with the Order, I want to help you."

"Okay," was all Ezio had said. He felt weird talking about the Hône Order with his dad. His dad was the one who had gotten him into this; sure, his father felt bad, but at the same time, he had signed Ezio's life away. There was no going back on that fifteen years later. It was too little too late, and Ezio was finding it hard to forgive his father.

"Yes," Tony said quietly. There was no one else home, but he still felt uneasy, fearing his wife would somehow hear him. Maya had no idea the Hône Order of Assassins existed, and Tony hoped to keep it that way.

"I need your help,"

Tony set down the fork that was in his hand and turned to face his son. Ezio wasn't sure how his father would react. Would he be helpful? Or would he chicken out and say no?

"What do you need?" Tony asked, trying his best not to sound reluctant, but his voice was strained.

"We need a ride up to Hône,"

"Why?"

"I have to talk to someone," Santos glanced at Ezio. It wasn't a total lie, but Ezio was blatantly leaving out the fact he was going to kill someone.

"Um, okay. Who are you going to talk to?"

"The leader of the Hône Order. A guy named Arcangelo."

"Ezio, Hône is over six hours away. I can't drive you there today. Your mom would ask questions—"

"Dad, I can't wait. Arcangelo killed or had someone else kill an assassin that was helping me."

"There was an assassin helping you?" Tony asked, his eyes wide. He was more bothered by his son talking with assassins rather than the fact he had witnessed someone get murdered.

"Yeah, a guy named Bernardo Moretti. He told me where to find Arcangelo, and that Arcangelo's the one who can stop all this. But we don't have a lot of time. I want to get this over with as quickly as possible."

"We need to think this through—"

"I already have. We go to Hône, Santos and I will go to the castle Arcangelo's in, and we'll deal with him. It'll be over in a matter of minutes."

"I'm not going to let you go in there alone,"

"Dad—"

"Ezio, I got you into this, I'm going to get you out." Tony said firmly. Ezio sighed through his nose.

"You're right, dad, you got me into this. You were the one who signed my life away thinking Angelo was just a senile old man. Well, dad, even if he *was* senile, why the hell would you ever agree to something like that? Why would you say, 'Oh yeah, make my son an assassin in sixteen years, I'm sure he won't mind?' Who *does* that?'"

Ezio hadn't realized how angry he was with his father. He had shouted at him, blustering, upset that his father had been so stupid to sign his unborn son's life away. *No sane man would ever do that!*

Tony was silent, and Ezio worried for a brief moment he had broken him. Maybe his father had felt guilty for the better part of fifteen years, knowing what he had done was wrong and praying every night that nothing would actually come of the promise he had made to Angelo Lombardi. But Ezio quickly dismissed that thought. At this point, his father was just as much of an enemy as Arcangelo. His father was the one who made the promise, not Arcangelo. Arcangelo was simply the crazy guy ready to execute the pact Tony and Angelo made. Tony could have said no to that pact, but he hadn't.

"I honestly didn't think Angelo was serious, Ezio. He's an old man! I thought he was so old he was harmless."

"Oh, that makes it all better," Ezio said sarcastically, the rage boiling inside of him. Santos stood beside him, feeling awkward standing in the middle of this shouting match. "An old man demands that your son becomes an assassin and then gives you that ring to make sure you never forget the pact. There's no way he could *possibly* be serious!" Tony glanced at the silver ring on his finger anxiously. The snake engraved on the band blinked at him in the dining room light, a constant reminder of his guilt and stupidity.

"I know it sounds stupid, but how was I supposed to know?" Tony was practically whispering. "I hadn't known he approached Sam, and I certainly didn't know he was an assassin."

"So what did you do when Sam told you?"

"I tried to talk to Angelo but he said it was too late. I didn't think he was going to keep his word, especially when he died! I thought he was really dead! I saw his body just like you did."

"You saw Edmondo Borteletti."

"Okay, Borteletti, whatever. But I thought it was Angelo, just like you did."

"That doesn't make up for the fact you were totally cool with signing me up to become an assassin!"

"I wasn't totally cool—"

"Yet you still did it,"

"Ezio, it's complicated!" Tony exclaimed. He didn't know how to explain his actions to his son. He didn't know how to explain them to himself. There was no justifying it anymore. "I'll drive you to Hône. I just don't know what to tell your mother."

"Tell her Don invited us to go fishing up north," Ezio said, mentioning his uncle Donatello. Don lived in Latina with his wife, Celeste, and their two sons, Dante and Nico. Dante was just a year younger than Ezio, and Nico was three years younger than Dante. They saw Donatello's family often, since they only lived an hour away.

"And if she asks Don about it?"

"It's mom we're talking about. She doesn't ask questions."

"But I do," a quiet voice behind Ezio and Santos said.

The two of them spun around, startled, and saw Marco standing in the kitchen, a grocery bag dangling from his hand. He had been at the store, getting some food for lunch while their mother and sisters were running other errands.

"What did you hear?" Tony asked, panicking. Ezio's anger disappeared, now being replaced with worry. What would Marco say? Would he tell their mother? Would he be angry at their dad too?

"Enough," Marco replied. "So Ezio's going to be an assassin, huh? How do we stop that?" Ezio glanced back at Tony, who was speechless. Marco wasn't acting at all as they had expected him to.

"Uh," Ezio began to answer. "We're driving up to Hône to talk with someone."

"Hône? Where's that?" Marco asked, setting the bag on the counter.

"Aosta Valley. Up north."

"When do we leave?"

"We?" both Ezio and Tony asked at the same time. Marco nodded.

"Yeah, the four of us. When do we leave?"

"Marco, I think it'd be best if it was just the three of us..." Tony said, his voice trailing off. Marco didn't blink.

"If you guys are going up against assassins, you're going to need all the help you can get. I'm going with you, and that's the end of it." The sixteen- going on seventeen-year-old began unpacking the groceries, lining them up neatly on the counter next to the bag. His birthday was in less than three weeks, and he was finishing up eleventh grade, leaving only one year before he graduated. Normal schools in Italy went up to grade thirteen, but not the International Academy of Italy. Students graduated a year earlier than traditional schools and went on to university at eighteen rather than nineteen.

"So when do we leave?" he asked again. Ezio and Santos looked back at Tony.

"I'll call your mother to tell her we're going to Don's, and then I'll make hotel reservations. We can leave after lunch and get up there around seven or eight."

CHAPTER SEVEN
ALL ROADS LEAD TO HÔNE

"Ah, Arcadia! I wasn't expecting you until next week!"

"Moretti's dead," Arcadia Conti said, not wasting any time with greetings. He was concerned for the group's well being. More importantly, he was concerned about the boy. "Killed by who I assume tried to kill me at the Palazzo Madama." Angelo Lombardi's expression darkened as he stared at the grey compound wall a few yards away.

"And Matteo?"

"At the safe house for now. I'm going to have him move soon, though."

"Do you think..." Angelo paused before continuing. "Do you think *he* was the one who hired the hit man?" *'He'* referred not to Matteo Conti, Arcadia's nephew, but to Arcangelo. The old man didn't want to say the name of the Order's leader, as if it had some sort of taboo on it.

"No doubt," Arcadia answered. He glanced up at the grey clouds in the distance. A storm would be coming this afternoon. "It's Tristan Clay. The same man he referred to you."

"Clay?" Angelo whispered the name, almost in disbelief. He had trusted Tristan at one point, but he should have known better. He should have known where the CIA agent's loyalty rested.

"What should we do?" Arcadia asked when the old man sitting in the green and yellow lawn chair said nothing more. He shook his head solemnly and adjusted the gardening hat on his head.

"Ezio," he began, then sighed, rubbing his temple anxiously. "Ezio will do what is necessary. Bernardo told him everything he needs to know. He will go to Hône. Please watch him and his friends for me. Keep them safe, Arcadia. Keep them safe."

*   *   *   *   *   *

It was a six and a half hour drive up to Aosta Valley from the Ferrari's house in perfect weather and traffic conditions, but when they got just an hour or so from Hône, near Novara, Piedmont, a snow storm began to brew, halting traffic on the A4 Torino-Trieste. The trip turned into an eight hour drive, the last two hours of which traffic was driven at less than thirty miles an hour.

It hadn't snowed in Rome in years, but in northern Italy, snow wasn't a rare sight. The freezing, slippery conditions that came with winter were not new to the

Ferraris—they had lived in Chicago, Illinois for over ten years, where it typically snowed from November to April, averaging 95 inches or so each year.

Santos, who had only seen snow two or three times in his life, if you didn't count movies or the Internet, was enthralled by the white, spinning blizzard.

"I thought it didn't snow in April," Marco commented as they drove at a snail's pace.

"Freak storm, I guess," Tony replied. He was sitting forward in his seat, gripping the steering wheel tightly as he kept his eyes glued to the road. Ezio noted his father was not driving as one normally should in these conditions; usually the driver kept their hands relaxed on the steering wheel in case the car began to spin on any ice. *He must be nervous*, he thought. But he doubted the nerves came from the weather.

The blizzard continued as they drove along the A4 Torino-Trieste and got onto the E25. Once they took the exit for the A5 heading toward Aosta, the storm let up slightly, and traffic began to move faster.

"So what's your plan, Ezio?" Tony asked as he took the roundabout onto the SS26. Ezio glanced at Santos. Neither of them had told Tony about killing

Arcangelo. But he had to know. It wasn't fair to keep him in the dark.

"I guess we'll eat dinner and then head over to the castle," Ezio replied slowly. He decided to just get it over with and tell him. "I, uh...I have to kill him." There was a stunned silence as Tony and Marco processed the information. Tony didn't take his eyes off the road, but the car did slow down a bit. Marco's mouth was hanging open as he stared out the windshield.

"I thought—"

"Yeah, I know, the whole point of me not becoming an assassin is so that I won't have to kill anybody. But apparently I have to kill Arcangelo. That's what Bernardo said."

"There isn't another way?" Tony asked, distraught at the idea of his son committing murder. He was very strongly opposed to the notion, and could hardly wrap his head around it.

"Not really. Dad, I know it's crazy and, you know, murder, but—"

"No," his father said. "You're not killing anybody." He said it as though Ezio had merely suggested punching Arcangelo like this was a schoolyard fight.

"There's no other way to get out of this. If there was, believe me, I'd do that instead."

"Why don't we wait until next year and deal with him then?" Tony asked, anxious Ezio was serious about killing someone.

"Because next year it'll be too late. No matter what we do, if we don't end it soon, Arcangelo will make me an assassin. The Order could take me today, or tomorrow, or next week—they can take me any time they want. But they'll take me on March 14 for sure."

"How do you know?" Marco said as he turned around in his seat to look at his brother.

"Bernardo told me. He knew everything about the Order's plan. He told me that I might not necessarily do anything, but just the fact that I'm listed as the leader of the Hône Order of Assassins will be enough to set things into motion. The assassins want to take over Italy, and they're going to use me to do it. The name 'Ezio' has a history behind it. An intimidating history. I'm supposedly going to be the best and most powerful assassin, and the reputation that precedes me already has the ball rolling. Parts of the Italian government know about me. Maybe not who I am or where I live, but they know about Ezio XXVII."

"Hold up, you're the twenty-seventh Ezio?" Tony asked. "I didn't know there were that many of you..."

"Yeah, neither did I. All the leaders of the Hône Order, except for this Arcangelo guy, are relatives of us. Angelo, your great uncle Renato—"

"My grandfather's twin brother was an assassin?" Tony's eyes were huge in the rearview mirror.

"Are you really surprised by that?" Ezio replied. His father said nothing.

"So they're going to use you to get to the government. Why can't they just do it on their own?" Marco asked. Ezio thought for a moment.

"Because Arcangelo doesn't want his name out there, he wants mine. There's this...rumor, from a long time ago, about how there would be an assassin named Ezio who would bring the Order back to its greatness. I am believed to be that Ezio. It's farfetched, but it's what the Order believes. It's why they want me."

"What if you turn out to be the crappiest assassin ever?"

"It doesn't matter. I'll still be used as a scapegoat. They just need my name slapped on the door that says, 'Leader of the Hône Order,' and the government will panic. Angelo was the last Ezio to be the leader, but he was kicked out. The government didn't really worry about Angelo since the CIA was watching him. His hands were tied. But the CIA doesn't know about me. They don't know I could be used to take down the Italian government. They don't really care. Italy's demise won't affect the United States."

No one said anything for a few minutes. It was a lot to handle, and it was confusing. Put simply, the Order just wanted Ezio's name, skills, and reputation. Everything else would just fall into place, and Italy would succumb to the Hône Order's renewed army.

"Can't we wait till tomorrow?" Marco finally asked with a yawn.

"Not really," Ezio said. "By tomorrow Arcangelo could know we're in town."

"So what? He can come try to kill us at the hotel. We could just take him down there, right?"

"Sure," Ezio said. "But I'd rather not have to deal with him at the hotel. The police would probably be called, and I don't think dad wants to get charged with murder in Hône when we're supposed to be at Lake Trasimeno." Tony's face grew red. He had told his wife that he was taking Marco, Milan, and Ezio to Lake Trasimeno in Umbria to go fishing with Donatello, Dante, and Nico. Fiona had wanted to go with her brothers, but Tony said no, that it was just a day trip for the boys. Maya had believed everything, and told them to have fun. Tony felt bad about lying, as did Ezio, but there was no other alternative.

Instead of Milan going with them, Santos took his place, telling his mom he was staying at Giovanni's house for the night. Milan pretended to be on the fishing trip while really going to Luke's apartment with Giovanni. They were lying to their parents once again, committing what they considered an elaborate scheme, just like they had back in June.

In the nine months since the boys' journey to Verona, not much had changed other than Milan moving in with the Ferraris. Their freshman year at the International Academy of Italy was almost over— there were nine weeks until the end of the term, and only five weeks before the start of final exams, which were spaced out over the course of twenty-eight days due to the number of students and classes at IAI. They were only in grade nine, which meant they had to take the International General Certificate for Secondary Education examinations. They were exams developed by the University of Cambridge that kids at the International Academy of Italy in grades nine and ten took. So, the boys focused on their schoolwork to prepare for the tests, and rarely spoke about what had happened over the summer. Occasionally, on their way home from school, the Hône Order would come up in Milan and Ezio's conversations, but other than that, they didn't talk about it. A small part of Ezio hoped, irrationally, that maybe if he didn't acknowledge the Order, then they would just go away. But he knew they wouldn't. Not unless he did something.

The Ferraris and Santos arrived at their hotel and parked out back. They walked into the lobby and went straight over to the check-in desk. Ezio didn't see Arcadia Conti watching from a bench as they checked in. He was drinking a complimentary espresso, keeping an eye on the group like Angelo had asked. As soon as they walked in, Arcadia pulled out his cell phone and called his friend.

"Hello?" Angelo said after a few rings. Something whirred loudly in the background. *Must be microwaving dinner*, Arcadia thought.

"How's the weather?" he asked, using the code phrase for "they're here." A woman sitting a few feet away glanced up from her magazine, but only for a second. Arcadia wondered briefly if she was working for the Order, but ultimately decided she wasn't. Arcangelo wouldn't have sent a subordinate assassin to deal with Ezio. He would have wanted to do it himself.

"And Arcangelo?" the old man's voice crackled through the speaker.

"The weather's clear here too," Arcadia replied, letting Angelo know that the leader hadn't shown up at the hotel.

"Where is Matteo?"

"He's doing well, thanks for asking. I believe he's renting a place across the street from the café."

"He's renting across from the Ferraris?"

"Yes, that's the place!" Arcadia said cheerfully.

At the check-in desk, Marco turned around and saw Arcadia. The rebel assassin held his breath as Marco made eye-contact with him. Did he know who he was? Did he recognize him? The teen's generally off-putting gaze seemed to pierce into Arcadia, studying him as he walked over. Arcadia had no idea Marco was thinking only about getting a free espresso from the stand next to the bench. The assassin, who typically never backed down from any challenge whatsoever, quickly glanced away. He couldn't draw attention to himself.

"That's the last place Arcangelo would look," Angelo was muttering to himself. The microwave beeped, and Arcadia heard him open and close the door. "I talked with Benito about him filling Bernardo's place."

"And?" Arcadia asked, feigning overdramatic interest as Marco stopped at the table next to him. He poured espresso from the coffee maker into a Styrofoam cup, grabbed a coffee stirrer, and began to walk away. Arcadia breathed a sigh of relief. The boy didn't know who he was.

"As much as he hates Ezio—he thinks he's a 'punk'—he hates Arcangelo more. He's willing to support us."

"Good," Arcadia said, not worried about code any longer. "That brings us back to four."

"It's still not enough," Angelo said as he took a bite of whatever he had been microwaving. "There's no way he and I can get to Hône soon enough to help with Arcangelo—"

"I wouldn't expect you to. It'd be an ideal opportunity for him to kill you both. I'll handle it." Arcadia rose from his seat as Tony took the room keys from the clerk. Just as Ezio turned around to follow his father to the elevators, Arcadia pushed through the glass doors of the lobby. He swiftly ducked around the side of the building as Angelo spoke again.

"Do you think they'll go tonight or tomorrow?"

"Tonight, most likely," he replied. "I'll go to the castle soon to keep an eye on them. Oh, and do you remember that Milan boy? The one Benito dealt with?"

"Yes, what about him?"

"He's going after Tristan Clay, along with Rizzo and Russell."

"I assume Matteo is following them?"

"No, I told Matteo to stay in the house, so he has a childhood friend tailing them. Said they met with a grey-haired man at the Colosseum and are scheduled to meet with Clay tonight at nine."

"Grey-haired man?" Angelo thought for a moment, rifling through the information contained in his mind, trying to find out if he knew who the boys' confidant was. His mental search achieved nothing. "Did Matteo's friend get pictures? Can we run a facial recognition?"

"No, but I'm sure I can find out who it is. Anyway, Matteo is watching Ezio's house to make sure Arcangelo doesn't send anyone after his family."

"Good. Thank you for your help."

"Don't thank me now," Arcadia muttered. "Ezio has yet to meet the live-in psycho of Hône."

CHAPTER EIGHT
ST. PETER'S SQUARE

The storm that the Ferraris and Santos had experienced in the Piedmont and Aosta Valley regions had reached the Lazio region in central Italy. This time, however, it was just a rain storm instead of a blizzard. The temperature had dropped into the low forties, and the boys' hoodies did little to protect them from the wet and cold. They stood huddled near the obelisk, St. Peter's Basilica looming behind them, their hands stuffed into their pockets and their hoods pulled up tightly around their heads in an effort to keep them warm.

"What time is it?" Luke asked, his teeth chattering. Milan pulled his cell phone out and shivered.

"Nine-fifteen," he replied, looking around the square. "Where is he?"

"I don't know. Didn't Gabriel say nine o'clock?" Luke said, shifting his weight.

"Yeah. I guess punctuality isn't one of Tristan Clay's strong suits."

"I say if he doesn't show up in the next ten minutes, we just head home and have Gabriel call the police." Giovanni said. Luke and Milan nodded in agreement. None of them wanted to stand out in the cold much longer.

"Hey, Giovanni, Luke!" a girl's voice suddenly echoed in the night air, instantly making this miserable night worse. In the dimly lit square, the boys could just make out the face of Sofia Greco, their classmate and Milan's enemy.

"Oh my God, what is *she* doing here?" Milan asked, not bothering to hide his disgust. He hated Sofia—she annoyed him and pretended he didn't exist. Over the summer, when the boys stopped in Rimini for a few hours before heading to Alessandria, Sofia had unfortunately been at the beach at the same time as them. She invited them to dinner, which was awkward, and since then, she only rarely talked to Luke, Giovanni, and Santos. She didn't like Ezio anymore because of what he had said to her about never playing sports during that awful dinner, but never said anything rude to him because of Marco's friendship with her sister.

"What are you guys doing here?" Sofia asked, her high pitched voice acting like a sword cutting through Milan's brain. She had on a pink rain coat, pink boots, and a pink umbrella. She reminded Giovanni of his six-year-old sister Ariana, who refused to wear any color other than pink.

"Uh..." Luke glanced at Giovanni. They couldn't tell her what they were really doing at the Vatican.

"We're just, um..."

"Working on our Italian project," Giovanni answered. "We were assigned to research the Basilica." The second part was true—Luke and Giovanni were working together on the project, just like Ezio and Santos were. Milan had been paired up with their friend Jack Wright, and Sofia had been paired with one of her friends.

"Oh, me and Renée were assigned the Pantheon," she replied. Renée Maçon was a French girl who had been at IAI longer than any of the boys. She was quiet and went along with whatever Sofia said or did—so if Sofia didn't talk to the boys, neither did Renée.

"Then why are you here?" Giovanni asked. He didn't have much patience for Sofia; he didn't like the way she treated his friends.

"We were just visiting the Basilica," she said. "My parents are getting the car."

"You're leaving? That's the best thing I've heard all day." Milan said. Sofia rolled her eyes and glared at him. He grinned at her. "Oh, I exist now?"

Without saying another word, Sofia turned briskly, walking toward the exit of the square. The boys grinned at each other, content she was gone.

"Now what time is it?" Luke asked, shivering again from the cold. Milan looked at his phone.

"Nine-twenty,"

"Can we just go? This guy—"

"Wait, is that him?" Giovanni interrupted, nodding towards a man, not much older than thirty, standing in between some pillars not too far from them.

A curly blonde-haired man in a brown jacket stood with his hands in his pockets, watching them. The boys glanced at each other and began to walk over to him. The man didn't move as they approached him, and instead watched them coolly.

"Are you Tristan?" Milan asked, standing up tall and pumping out his chest to make himself seem older than fourteen and a half. The man didn't move.

"Who are you?" he asked. He had been contacted by a grown man—not a bunch of kids.

"I'm Milan. This is Giovanni and Luke." The man studied the boys, deciding whether or not to trust them. The obvious leader of the small group was the one speaking; he was relatively tall, with tan skin and chocolate colored hair. He looked Hispanic, and spoke with a slight New York accent. The second boy, who was a little taller than the frontman, had timid brown eyes and looked Italian. His dark hair was almost invisible under the hood of his navy blue sweatshirt, swept back away from his forehead. The third boy was significantly different from the other two, not only in height but also in appearance. He was short, not much more than five foot four, with sand-colored hair and blue eyes. He was an odd character; he had the face of a bored teenager yet broke into a mischievous grin easily. He looked slightly younger than the other two, but in reality, Luke Russell was older than all of his friends by a range of one to six months.

"We need to talk," Milan continued when Tristan didn't say anything, assuming he was, in fact, Tristan Clay. "What do you know about the Hône Order of Assassins?" He wanted to get this over with. He was cold and tired and was beginning to regret agreeing to this meeting. *I should have gone with Ezio and Santos instead*, he thought.

"Easy there, tiger," Tristan answered as though Milan was a little kid asking for cookies before dinner. "I'm not saying anything until I get my money."

"Money?" Milan and Giovanni said at the same time. Gabriel hadn't told them anything about money.

"Yeah, my money. The guy who called my hotel room said you'd have a briefcase." He peered around Giovanni at Luke. "And I don't see any briefcase."

"Uh," Milan glanced at his friends. "We weren't told you wanted money." Tristan snorted.

"What is this?" he asked, not able to understand why there were *kids* standing in front of him.

"We need answers," Luke said with quiet confidence. "About why you were going to kill Arcadia Conti."

"I'm not talking till I get my money." Tristan repeated, standing his ground and crossing his arms. He was running a huge risk meeting in a public place —money was the only thing that would compensate for that.

"Look, buddy, we just want to know what you know about the Hône Order of Assassins." Milan said, impatient with Clay's stubbornness. The agent considered this for a moment.

"I know you don't want to get involved with them and I know I'm not your buddy, *pal*," he answered with a harsh glare. Milan didn't blink.

"We're already involved with them. We just want to know what the CIA knows."

"The CIA has outdated information," the man replied simply. Milan shifted his weight anxiously. It seemed to be getting colder, and he didn't want to deal with Tristan's games.

"How are you involved with the Order?" Luke asked quickly, sensing Milan's frustration. Tristan looked as if he wouldn't answer, but then said:

"I was assigned to watch for threats from organized crime groups in Italy—namely, the Hône Order of Assassins," he said robotically, just in case the kids had recording devices on them to give to the police. He was, after all, a very wanted man for many different reasons now.

"And?"

"You'll get more information when I get my money," Tristan said.

"We already told you, we didn't know you wanted money—"

"Then I guess this meeting's over," Tristan said, beginning to walk away.

"Wait—" It was no use. The man was walking away, and it was quite evident he would not be turning around. The trio stood still, unsure of what to do next, the sound of rain pouring down from the clouds and police sirens off in the distance doing little to aid their thoughts.

"You guys blew that," a startling voice from behind the boys said. They turned around and saw Gabriel standing behind them in the shadows.

"*We* blew it? You were the one that told him we'd have money, which we clearly *don't have*." Milan said angrily. "Why would you say that?" Gabriel didn't answer. Instead, he walked forward, following Tristan toward the Sistine Chapel.

Through the roar of the pouring rain, Tristan heard footsteps following him. He turned and saw Gabriel, and his eyes grew wide.

"You're Hunter," he gasped, and at first, Milan thought he said it in admiration. But then he realized, as Tristan kept backing away, that he was scared.

"Yeah, and you're Clay," Gabriel replied in his deep, whispery voice.

"You went rogue,"

"So did you,"

"We were told you went off the deep end." Tristan was still backing away, inching closer and closer to the Chapel.

"I probably did," Gabriel said, his low voice somehow cutting through the rain. "But this isn't about me. This is about you, and these kids. You tell them what they need to know, and this will all be over."

"But I didn't get my—"

"Forget the money!" Gabriel said, exasperated. "What is it with you younger agents? All you care about is money. Just answer the questions before the police show—" Gabriel stopped himself, but not soon enough. Tristan heard the word "police" and bolted toward the entrance of St. Peter's Square. "Great," he muttered, chasing after the CIA agent. The boys followed suit, their feet splashing in puddles.

"Did you call them already?" Giovanni called to Gabriel.

"They're on their way," he answered. "If I were you I'd get out of here."

The boys stopped running and looked at each other. They were a few feet from the obelisk, the tall pointed monument hiding them in a shadow of darkness. The sirens they had heard earlier were getting closer, and down the street the first of many red and blue lights were flashing.

"Come on," Milan said. He didn't want to be around when the police showed up.

They walked to the edge of St. Peter's Square and turned right, heading in the direction of the Trevi Fountain and their neighborhood. But as they were walking away from Vatican City, the cops blocked off the street Tristan was running down.

There was shouting as the boys kept their backs turned, pretending as if they had no idea the cops were just one street over. There was no one else on the road, but there were security cameras all around to protect the pope from criminals and religious fanatics.

The boys turned around, though, when they heard the unmistakable sound of gunshots muffled by the rain. They dashed to the corner of a building, heading toward the gunshots instead of away, and looked at the scene that had unfolded just seconds before. There was someone laying on the ground, with several police officers walking towards him, their guns drawn.

In the arc of one of the street lamps, it was clear the body belonged to that of the curly haired agent. The boys stared at each other in horror. The man in the street lamp had been shot by the police. In the blink of an eye, Tristan Clay was dead.

CHAPTER NINE
THE LIVE-IN PSYCHO

After a quick dinner ordered from the restaurant on the first floor of their hotel and a phone call to check in with Maya, Tony, Marco, Santos, and Ezio went outside into the freezing cold and climbed into the car. Tony pulled away from the hotel and told the kids to look around for castles. They had no address for the Hône Order's former headquarters, so it was just a guessing game.

"Do you think he's in Fort Bard?" Marco asked, referencing the castle in the next town over. They were driving slowly down the narrow street the hotel was situated on, searching for what could be the home of the Hône Order. Ezio shook his head from the backseat.

"No, that's a museum now. Besides, Fort Bard is in *Bard*, not Hône."

"Just a suggestion," Marco muttered. Santos suddenly sat upright and pointed out the window.

"There, by the lake! Is that a castle?"

Off in the distance, situated on the top of a tall, snow covered hill, was a four-story high castle made of stone and concrete. A few lights illuminated windows that lined the walls evenly. Ezio and Santos looked at each other. It was the only castle in Hône that they'd found so far.

"It's worth a try,"

Tony steered the car in the direction of the castle, secretly hoping Ezio and Santos were wrong about the castle being the former headquarters. He had a bad feeling about this meeting with Arcangelo, and regretted driving the boys to Hône. He should have put his foot down and refused, but he hadn't. Why hadn't he? *This is crazy,* he thought to himself. *This is just asking for one of us to get hurt, or killed. Why did I agree to this?*

Tony pulled into a parking lot at the bottom of the hill. The four of them got their coats and boots from the trunk and prepared for their trek up the steep landmass.

"We're really walking all the way up there? We can't just park in the driveway or something?" Marco asked, looking at the hill distastefully. Ezio was sitting in the backseat, his legs dangling out the side of the car, and tugged on his boots. He looked at the hill, then at his brother.

"What's the problem?" he asked.

"The castle's like, a mile away. Uphill." Ezio shrugged.

"I'd say half a mile at most."

"Not my point," Marco said. "My point is, it seems like a lot of unnecessary walking. We'll be tired by the time we get up there, and then how are we supposed to fight Arcangelo?"

"We'll be fine," Ezio reassured his brother, hopping out of the car.

They had come fairly prepared for their journey with ski jackets, boots, hats, and gloves—all of which Tony had to dig out of the basement since they hadn't used them since they visited Chicago the previous year. Santos was borrowing a jacket of Marco's that he had grown out of, but that Santos fit in perfectly.

Ezio slipped on the hidden blade when no one was looking, pulling the sleeve of his sweatshirt over it. It was a little big on him, just like Bernardo said, but it wouldn't slip off unless he pulled on it.

After getting bundled up, the four of them set off for the castle. It was -1° Celsius, or 29° Fahrenheit, much colder than normal for Hône this time of year. There was a biting wind that made their hike more miserable than it was already going to be. The only good thing, that Ezio could find, was that it had stopped snowing.

They trudged slowly north up the hill, taking their time. They were in no hurry to meet *Arcangelo Della*

Morte. The castle sat at the top, beckoning them. Ezio wondered if Arcangelo knew they were in Hône. Was he waiting for them?

The frigid wind blew in their direction, attacking them through their heavy coats like daggers made of ice. Snow drifted up from the ground and was whipped into their faces by the wind. Their skin stung from the cold, and visibility was occasionally reduced significantly when the snow was picked up. They kept their heads down as a futile attempt to protect themselves in any way possible. Ezio glanced up every so often to see how far away the lights of the fortress were. They were getting closer—slowly.

The hill was covered with at least three feet of snow, if not more. This made it very difficult to maneuver in, and their feet felt frozen even in their boots. The group thought they were prepared for their winter hike—but they had no idea how arctic the temperatures would be when they left Rome.

This weather phenomenon was unusual, especially for early April. Winter was typically over by now, and spring would be starting. Hône was not deep in the mountainous Aosta Valley, so it didn't always snow this much or get this cold. But the winter season all over Italy had been colder and a little longer than normal.

People in central Italy weren't used to prolonged periods of cold, and were upset that in April, the weather had done little to clear up. Meteorologists reassured the people of central and southern Italy, who were used to a Mediterranean climate, that this was a fluke season and would not happen again for a while. But right now, it was happening, and it sucked.

After what felt like hours of battling the freezing snow and wind, they finally reached the castle. It was bigger than it had looked from the parking lot below; it was four stories high and seemed to go on endlessly. Angelo Lombardi's house had seemed never-ending, but this castle made it look puny. The house had only been one-story and had an awkward, maze-like layout. This was just a very large fortress.

"Now what?" Santos asked when they reached the top of the hill. Ezio scanned the façade of the castle. A few windows were lit, but the rest were dark. There was one window, several yards away, that appeared to be opened just a little.

Ezio's first thought was that it was strange a window would be open on such a terribly cold night. Not only was the heat inside the castle escaping through the window, making the room colder, but the heating bill would be enormous! If Arcangelo had any economic sense at all, surely he would have kept the window shut...

But then Ezio realized the window had not been left open as a source of fresh air, but as a means for him to enter. Arcangelo was expecting him to show up. Was he expecting him to have the hidden blade Bernardo had given him? Ezio could feel the brace clinging loosely to his skinny wrist beneath the heavy jacket. Would he really use it when the time came?

"There's a window over there," Ezio nodded toward it, knowing he was going to be leading them all into a trap. Who knew what would be waiting for them on the other side of the stone wall?

They laboriously walked to the window, which was open just enough to be visible, but not enough for anyone to fit through. It was one of those windows that pushes out, acting as a sort of awning to shield the room from the elements, even if just a little.

Ezio pulled the window out farther so they could climb through it. He went in first, just in case Arcangelo was in the room. He was the only one with a weapon. Santos followed, with Marco and Tony after him.

The room was small and cramped. It was a bathroom, but it only had a toilet and a sink. The door was wide open, and led into a large corridor. The four of them stepped over the threshold and were amazed at what they saw.

The ceiling was thirty-feet tall, with grey rock arches. The corridor was lit by dozens of burning torches, spaced equally apart from each other. Huge, dark, oak doors stood at one end of the hall, to the left of the bathroom. Ezio assumed they led outside. The floor was carpeted with red velvet, and small ornate paintings decorated the walls along with the torches. The four of them removed their jackets and walked around for a minute, warming up and admiring the grandeur that was the foyer of the castle.

Marco stepped over to one of the paintings. It was a small rectangle of parchment paper fitted onto a smooth wooden board not much bigger. On the parchment paper was a painting of Jesus. Marco smirked.

"He's got an icon of Jesus. How ironic," he said.

"I am a man of faith," a voice above them echoed. Ezio's heart jumped to his throat. He turned and saw a man standing on a balcony overlooking the foyer, his hands on the rail supported by ivory banisters. Two large, winding staircases led up to the balcony. Behind the man was a hallway; on either side of that hallway were more staircases. Marco glanced at Ezio. Even though neither of them had ever seen the Archangel of Death, something made them think this was him.

"How does a man of God kill so many people?" Ezio asked. There were a dozen religious icons adorning the foyer walls. Arcangelo's seriousness about religion seemed to contradict his occupation.

"I sleep just fine, if that's what you were asking," the assassin replied with a smile. Ezio hadn't been asking, but he decided to let it go. He wasn't going to engage Arcangelo in childish banter.

"You know why I'm here, right?" he asked. Arcangelo knew everything there was to know about Ezio. Surely he would know why he was at the castle.

"You're here to kill me."

The way Arcangelo said it was mocking, as if he knew Ezio wouldn't go through with it. And hearing Arcangelo's mockery only made Ezio feel weaker and more helpless. He had thrown up when Bernardo, a man he barely knew, had died. How could he possibly take another man's life? To watch the light fade from his eyes and know that he was the one who extinguished it...he felt queasy just thinking about it. Upon seeing the mixed emotions on the boy's face, Arcangelo continued.

"I'll make a deal with you, Ezio. If you kill me, you won't have to become an assassin. I won't be here to force you into the Order. But if you don't kill me...well, your birthday won't be a very happy day, now will it?"

It was a simple deal. One that, if Ezio didn't have a conscience, would have been easy to take part in. Ezio was torn. He didn't want to kill Arcangelo, but he didn't want to be an assassin. Arcangelo stared down at him, waiting for an answer. His dad, brother, and friend were watching him too. Ezio couldn't think with all these people staring at him. It didn't help Jesus was watching him from his plaque.

"What if I don't take the deal at all?" Ezio asked, wondering if maybe he'd found a loop hole. Arcangelo didn't hesitate.

"If you don't take this deal, then I suppose I won't waste any more of your time. You'll stay here and become an assassin. And if you comply, I'll let the others go free. How does that sound?" Ezio said nothing at first. Then, quietly, afraid of hearing his own voice say the words, he said: "Deal."

"May the best man win," Arcangelo said, smiling kindly, patronizing him. This was all a game to him. He turned around and walked down the hall behind him, his footsteps echoing through the foyer. A door opened and closed. Then there was silence.

No one said anything. No one moved. Outside, everything was still and quiet. Peaceful. The calm before the storm. Ezio looked over at his dad. Tony stared at his son, and he felt as though his heart was shattering into a million little pieces as he saw the look in Ezio's eyes. The pleading, frightened brown eyes that already looked remorseful, before he had even done anything.

"Dad," Ezio spoke the single word, his voice cracking. He said nothing more. He couldn't. Tony shook his head.

"I understand," he whispered. Ezio looked at Marco and Santos. They nodded solemnly. Ezio turned and pulled his sleeve up slightly and saw the brace. The blade hidden beneath, retracted, waiting for its chance to kill. Ezio pressed the button and the blade slid out in the blink of an eye, without a sound, reflecting the torch light. He pressed the button again, concealing it, and started forward toward the stairs.

"Wait," Marco said, going over to his brother. "I'll go with you."

"Marco, it's—"

"Something you have to do yourself. I know. But I'm not letting you get all the action." The boys looked back at their dad, who didn't seem to condone nor object to Marco's idea. Ezio nodded, and together, the two brothers ascended the stairs.

CHAPTER TEN
NERO LAGORIO

Ezio dug the dagger out of his boot and gave it to Marco. He had stolen it from Angelo's arsenal back in June, and had thought it might come in handy during their expedition to Hône. Marco held it tentatively in his hand. He looked at his little brother.

"Just in case," Ezio said.

They walked down the hall Arcangelo had disappeared into minutes before. They passed portraits of what were considered modern Order leaders. The paintings hung on the left wall; on the right there were six doors. Five of the doors were wide open, showing no sign of Arcangelo. The second to last door, though, was closed. Marco and Ezio silently agreed that Arcangelo must be in that room, and came to the decision Ezio would go in first, with Marco right behind him. *Maybe if Arcangelo sees it's two against one, he'll just give up,* Ezio thought. He knew it was a long shot, but he prayed he would be right.

He turned the brass knob and pushed the door open. He stepped in the room and opened his mouth to say something, but stopped. Something was flying through the air, heading straight towards him. He ducked to the right, but it was a second too late. The large object, which was attached to a cord, hit the left half of his face, knocking him to the ground and sending him into unconsciousness.

When he came to, Marco was kneeling over him, saying something Ezio couldn't quite understand. His brother was in and out of focus, and at times there seemed to be two of him.

"What happened?" Ezio finally mumbled, propping himself up on his elbows.

"You got knocked out," Marco said with an anxious grin.

"How long was I out?" he groaned, rubbing his bruised face. His cheek and forehead were throbbing, and he could feel his left eye beginning to swell.

"Four minutes or so," Marco replied. "How soon do you think you can walk?" Ezio held out his hand for Marco to help him up. As soon as he was vertical, he felt dizzy, but was strong enough to stay upright.

"Did you find Arcangelo?" Ezio asked. Marco hesitated.

"Well, not exactly..." he said. "After you got knocked out, I ran to get dad. He was on the floor, I guess Arcangelo snuck up on him somehow and hit him on the head pretty hard. I couldn't find Santos. Dad doesn't know what happened to him or where he went." Ezio sighed and looked around the room they were in.

"Where's dad now?" he asked, stepping over to a desk that stood in the middle of the floor.

"He went to look for Santos,"

"Okay. For now we need to assume that Arcangelo took Santos and he's in danger. We need to pretend dad's missing, and that we're on our own."

"Why?" Marco asked.

"Because that's the worse case scenario. And who knows, that could be the scenario we're in right now." Ezio began to open the drawers of the desk, not sure what he was looking for. But he would know what it was when he found it.

*   *   *   *   *   *

721 kilometers south of Hône, *Ispettore Capo* Nero Lagorio was standing under a black umbrella outside St. Peter's Square. The rain poured down around him, the loud *tap-tap-tap* of the droplets on the taut fabric doing little to interrupt his train of thought. He held in his hand a picture of the man his officers had shot. The department had received an anonymous tip from a pay phone near the square, identifying the

shooter from the Palazzo Madama as Tristan Clay, and informing the desk clerk that Clay was currently at the Vatican. The operator had asked the caller how he knew this information, but he did not answer her and just hung up.

"*Come le pare che stia?*" What do you think, sir? Lagorio's *Vice Ispettore* Placido Abate asked. Officers milled around the street, looking for evidence and talking to the two witnesses, a priest and a woman who had been walking her dog after dinner.

"*Non saprei,*" I'm not sure, Lagorio muttered, studying the witnesses from a distance. "*Ritorno in centrale per fare delle indagini su questo tizio Tristan Clay. Chiamami se scopri qualcosa.*" I'm going back to the station to do some research on this Tristan Clay man. Call me if you find anything.

Lagorio walked briskly to his car, passing impatient police officers doing their jobs grudgingly. It was almost ten o'clock, and the officers were working overtime, missing dinner with their families. Lagorio didn't mind working overtime—he had no reason to rush home, no one waiting for him to sit down at the dinner table—and this particular case intrigued him. A CIA agent attempted to kill the President of the Senate? What a scandal! He couldn't wait to see the headlines in the paper the next morning. This was exciting stuff.

The police station was practically deserted when Lagorio arrived. He went to his office and sat down at his desk, switched on the little light he had sitting there, and typed Tristan Clay's name into a search engine. Nothing came up, but that was no surprise to Lagorio. Clay was a CIA agent. His life was a secret.

So instead, Lagorio picked up the phone and dialed the number for the CIA liaison to Italy. It rang and rang, and Lagorio wondered why no one was picking up. It was only four o'clock in the afternoon in America. But then, the voicemail answered his question, in both English and Italian.

"Hello, this is Tristan Clay with the American CIA, official liaison to Italy. Please leave a message and I will get back to you as soon as possible. Thank you." *Salve, sono Tristan Clay della CIA Americana e intermediario ufficiale per l'Italia. Lasciate un messaggio e vi richiamerò appena possibile. Grazie.*

Lagorio hung up the phone and looked up the number for United Nations. A woman at the New York City headquarters answered.

"Hello, United Nations," she said, sounding very rehearsed. "How may I help you?"

"Hello, my name is Chief Inspector Nero Lagorio with the State Police in Italy, and I am looking to get in touch with the Central Intelligence Agency." The woman on the other line hesitated.

"Why?" she asked.

"Because I have reason to believe that an agent of theirs is involved with a crime that was committed yesterday afternoon. Do you mind connecting me with the CIA?"

"Uh, one moment please," Lagorio waited patiently. "Did you contact the CIA liaison to Italy?" she asked a few seconds later.

"I did,"

"What did he say?"

"He was of no use to me," Lagorio replied. This woman didn't need to know the liaison was involved.

"Well he is the one who—"

"I know, he is the one who I am supposed to speak with. But he cannot help me. I need to speak with the Italian liaison's superior."

"One moment please," Lagorio heard himself being connected to another phone line. A minute later, someone picked up.

"Karen Thompkins, head of foreign diplomacy with the CIA, how may I help you?"

"Hello, Ms. Thompkins, I am Chief Inspector Nero Lagorio with the State Police in Rome. I was wondering what you can tell me about one of your agents named Tristan Clay?" There was silence. Lagorio waited.

"Why, has something happened to him?" Karen asked.

"I'm afraid so,"

"Can you elaborate?'"

"I need you to tell me what Mr. Clay was doing in Rome,"

"He was on vacation," Karen replied. "He was going to be dismissed soon and needed to use up his vacation days. Now what happened to Agent Clay?'"

"My officers shot him about—" Lagorio glanced at the clock. "—forty-six minutes ago. He drew a weapon on us and is believed to have attempted to kill the President of the Senate, Aurelio Conti." Karen sighed.

"Great, another international scandal we have to deal with. We'll send over a couple of agents tomorrow morning. Thank you for calling, Inspector Lagorio. You have our full cooperation."

"Thank you, Ms. Thompkins. Have a good afternoon."

Lagorio hung up the phone and got ready to go home. As he was walking towards the front door, he left a note on Abate's desk:

The CIA is sending two agents tomorrow. Make sure you pull the security footage from St. Peter's Square. I have reason to believe Clay was not alone.

*　　*　　*　　*　　*　　*

Ezio lifted a large book from one of the drawers of Arcangelo's desk. It was a dusty brown color, leather bound, and the title on the front cover was so faded he couldn't decipher it. He set it down on the desk and opened it.

Marco peered over his shoulder, reading the same words with his brother. When they both finished the first paragraph, which was neatly handwritten in Italian, they looked at each other.

"This is a history book," Marco said.

"Yeah, a history of the Hône Order of Assassins," Ezio began flipping through the pages. It was a very detailed account of everything the Hône Order had gone through and done since 1100. But on the last four pages, there was a list.

"What is that?" Marco asked.

"It's a list of all the leaders," Ezio replied, flipping to the last page. "Starting with Aetos I and ending with me." Next to every leader was the year of their birth and the year of their death. Starting in the 1900s, the middle name of each leader was written to better identify them. For the last three leaders, there was no year of death, meaning they were still alive. And next to the second to last leader, there was an asterisk.

Ezio XXV – Angelo   1937

_____

*Ezio XXVI   1952

_____

Ezio XXVII – Enzo 1999

_____

_____

*Honorable leader, not a descendent of
Aetos I

"Are we related to Aetos I?" Marco asked. Ezio nodded.

"Everyone in this book is related to Aetos I except for Arcangelo,"

"So we're related to *all* those assassins?" Ezio nodded again. *Hopefully Angelo's the last assassin in our family*, he thought.

CHAPTER ELEVEN
THE TUNNELS

Ezio and Marco went down to the foyer and stashed the book underneath their coats. From there, they began walking through the first floor of the castle. The layout wasn't nearly as confusing as Angelo's house, but the corridors were long, and every so often there would be a hall that branched off. There seemed to be hundreds of rooms. *Why would anyone ever need this much space?*

"This is hopeless," Marco said, exasperated. "This place is huge. We're never going to find anyone in this place."

"It's got to end sometime, right? The castle doesn't go on infinitely. We'll find them. They didn't just vanish."

"Yeah, but what if we're looking in all the wrong places?"

"We'll have to look in the right places eventually," Marco stopped arguing and stayed quiet for a while. Then suddenly, he stopped.

"Do you hear that?" he asked quietly. Ezio stopped and listened. There was a muffled voice nearby.

"Sounds like Arcangelo," Ezio whispered. Marco nodded in agreement.

"Where do you think he is?" Ezio stepped forward quietly, listening carefully for a fluctuation in the noise level. They were getting closer.

He motioned for Marco to follow him, and together they crept forward. There was a closed door nearby that seemed to contain the voice behind it. Ezio hesitated. What if this was a trap again? What if something came flying at his face again? That would really annoy him.

Ezio was just about to open the door when he remembered the hidden blade. He pressed the button and the blade slid out, almost completely inaudible. But just as the blade slid out, the voice behind the door stopped talking. Ezio froze. He and Marco glanced at each other, neither of them willing to even breathe. No sound was made on the other side of the door. Had Arcangelo somehow heard the blade?

That would be impossible. The blade slid out so quietly you wouldn't be able to hear it unless you were listening for it. And Arcangelo had been talking— there was no way he could have heard it.

But he had. The door swung open, taking Ezio's arm with it, since his hand had been on the doorknob. Ezio stumbled forward and was met by an uppercut to the jaw. It took him off guard and he stumbled to one side. Arcangelo pushed him, a wild look in his eyes, as if he really thought Ezio was going to kill him. He shoved Marco out of the way and took off running down the hall.

"Go!" Ezio yelled to his brother, scrambling to his feet.

He and Marco chased after Arcangelo, not thinking for a minute that this could be another trap. They followed Arcangelo down a flight of stairs, and then another, until they were two floors underground. There were no windows and it was significantly colder down here, and darker, with fewer torches lighting the hallways. Arcangelo disappeared into another corridor. The boys followed without hesitation.

The boys only realized Arcangelo could be baiting them when something struck Marco's shoulder.

"Ow!" he yelled out in pain. He looked down and saw something sticking out of his right shoulder. "Oh my God I got stabbed!" Ezio whipped around and peered through the dim light. He could see the hilt of a dagger sticking out of his brother.

"Run," Ezio said, shoving him back the way they came. "Don't pull it out yet."

"I kind of don't want to!"

Something clipped Ezio's right ear, and he felt blood dripping from it. He knew Arcangelo was throwing daggers at them, much like Angelo Lombardi had. The difference was Angelo was careful not to hurt them; Arcangelo *wanted* to hurt them.

The boys dashed into another corridor in an attempt to distance themselves from Arcangelo, and Ezio realized these were not, in fact, hallways. They were in a series of intricate tunnels. The walls and ceiling were one, forming an oblong tube. There were more tunnels branching off sporadically from the one they were in—like a maze. *What is it with assassins and crappy floor plans?*

Ezio and Marco ran as fast as they could for as long as they could. They didn't stop until they felt sure they had lost Arcangelo. And even then, they kept moving. They walked until their breathing had regulated and they hadn't heard any more noises from nearby tunnels. Ezio took this lapse in action as an opportunity to examine the tunnels more closely. Wooden crates stood at random increments alongside the walls. They were unmarked and sealed tightly, making it impossible for anyone to know what was inside without prying them open. Ezio glanced over at Marco, about to suggest they open one of the boxes, but then noticed the dagger protruding from his brother.

"How's your shoulder?" he asked, trying to be casual.

"I don't know, it has a knife in it," Marco answered sarcastically. "What are we supposed to do? We're not doctors, we don't know how to handle these types of situations!" Ezio took a look at his brother's injury. The blade hung loosely from his shoulder, the hilt pointing downward. The cut was bad, but luckily because of all the running Marco had done, the blade had become dislodged and was closer to the surface than before.

"Relax, it's almost out on its own," Ezio said, grabbing the hilt and pulling.

"Ow! Stop!" Marco said, swatting his hand away. Ezio grinned, holding the knife in his hand.

"All better," he said. "Want a bandage?"

"Yeah, you got one on you?" Marco asked, knowing they hadn't come prepared for injuries. But he was smiling out of relief, which was a good sign. Ezio shook his head and took off his hoodie. He handed it to Marco.

"Hold this," he said. He removed his shirt and ripped part of it off. He put his ragged shirt on again and took his hoodie back.

"Wrap that around the cut tight so there's pressure on it," he advised. Marco did as he was told and looked at his brother.

"How'd you know to do that?" Ezio shrugged.

"I guess I just knew it. Must've picked it up from somewhere."

As the two of them walked through the tunnels, Ezio felt his ear. It was wet with blood, but he determined only the top part of his ear had been cut. There would be no permanent damage. *Marco, on the other hand, might have a scar for a few years, if not life.*

From the tunnels, Ezio and Marco could hear shouting. They didn't know how near they were, or if they were even on their level, but they recognized the voice. It was their dad.

The boys began to run, hoping to find their father, wherever he was. They didn't want Tony to go up against Arcangelo alone, especially since they knew he was armed and ruthless.

"Look around for a stairwell or something. We need to get back up top." Ezio told his brother. Their footsteps echoed through the dark, damp, cold tunnels that snaked beneath the castle. Stalactites clung to the ceiling, pointed at the end like the daggers that had just been thrown at them. Water dripped from the stalactites onto the cobblestone path the brothers were running on, forming the puddles their feet splashed in.

"In here," Marco said, darting down a narrow corridor with a light at the end of it. "This has to be the way out, right?"

Ezio followed him, heart racing, his stomach flip-flopping uncontrollably no matter how much he tried to calm himself. They had lost Arcangelo several turns ago—why was he still afraid?

"Wait, Marco," Ezio called, his voice echoing off the walls of the side tunnel. Marco slowed to a stop and turned around. "Think about it. The rest of this tunnel is either dark or barely lit at all, yet that room is really bright? Plus there's no stairwell over there. How could that be the way out?" Marco glanced back at the light, which was a rectangle the size of a door just twenty feet away.

"Maybe there are stairs, but we just can't see them," he said.

"I don't know. I just have a bad feeling about it."

"Let's just check it out anyway. If it doesn't lead anywhere, we'll turn around and keep going the way we were."

Ezio didn't like it, but he walked alongside his brother toward the light. Eighteen feet...sixteen feet...fourteen...Ezio noticed that as the light got closer, it shifted. It was *moving*.

"Marco, stop," he said. Something was wrong. Ezio looked up at the ceiling, which was dotted with dripping stalactites. He held out his hand and caught a couple drops of the clear liquid as they fell. He sniffed the droplets. Something wasn't right about them. They smelled weird. Next, he tasted them, and spat immediately in disgust. His suspicion was confirmed.

"Kerosene," he told his brother. "We have to get out—"

It was too late. The rectangle of light burst through the room it had been contained in, exploding forward and gaining energy as it touched the kerosene coated floor. The heat washed over them, and instantly, Ezio broke out in a sweat. He and Marco stumbled backward, shocked at first, but they quickly recovered.

"Come on!" Ezio screamed, grabbing his brother's arm. They retreated back to the main tunnel, the flames licking at their heels and gaining on them, spreading quickly across the kerosene.

"What is it with these assassins and fire?" Ezio shouted, sprinting into the main tunnel.

This was the second time within forty-eight hours that Ezio had been in danger of death by fire. He had already suffered from smoke inhalation, and that was painful enough. He didn't want to start coughing uncontrollably again.

"In here," Ezio said, pushing his brother ahead of him into another corridor. The fire was spreading up and down both ends of the tunnel. Soon, the flames would use up all the oxygen, and the underground death-trap would become completely filled with smoke. It wouldn't be long before he and Marco suffocated.

"This is backwards," Marco said, stopping suddenly. Ezio looked at him wildly.

"This is no time to be overprotective. Hurry up!"

"Yeah but what if—"

"We don't have time for 'what if.' Come on!"

The flames found them in their corridor, rejoicing over the fact they had more fuel. All traces of overprotectiveness left Marco; he ran forward, sprinting ahead of his little brother. Ezio followed him, his throat already starting to burn.

"There's some stairs!" Marco exclaimed, pointing at a short staircase about forty feet ahead of them. They ran with a new found speed, their hearts pounding, throats burning, eyes stinging. The fire licked at their heels, taunting them, letting them know it was still there. Marco ran up the stairs, five uneven cobblestone steps, and tried the heavy wooden door that was in the wall at the top. It wouldn't budge.

"What now?" Marco asked frantically, tears involuntarily streaming down his face. Ezio tried the door, but it still wouldn't budge. The flames were slowing, slightly — there weren't as many stalactites in this room as in the tunnel — but they were still inching closer and closer.

Ezio lifted the dagger that had been stuck in Marco's shoulder, wiped the blood off of it, and jammed it into the lock beneath the door knob. He twisted it, praying it would work. It didn't.

CHAPTER TWELVE
EXPENDABLE

"Ezio," Marco said, the terror in his voice quite evident.

"Gimme a second," his brother said, turning the dagger again. He heard a faint click, and felt the door give way a little.

"Go!" He shoved Marco through the door and followed suit. He shut the heavy wooden door behind them just as the flames reached his ankles.

"Oh my God," Marco was shaking. They had almost died.

"We need to get out of here," Ezio said, stating the obvious. The flames would eat through the door in a matter of minutes; they had time, but would it be enough?

"Ezio," Marco said as his brother examined the tiny room they were in. It seemed like some kind of storage closet. "What the hell is going on? I thought they wanted you—"

"I'm expendable," Ezio answered. The notion had come to him just now. Everything added up—the object that hit him in the head, the daggers being thrown at them, the fire—and Ezio was beginning to realize *how* he was expendable. "I'm *convenient*. I make the Hône Order's goal easier to achieve. But I don't make their objective *possible*. Arcangelo makes that possible. I'm the guy who will take the blame. I'll be the guy other governments will have killed. I'm the guy to draw attention from Arcangelo. If I die, they can still go through with their plans. It's just a matter of finding a replacement and changing his name. Any Ezio will do. They can lie, but only if I'm dead. Because if I'm dead, I can't dispute them or try to stop them. Arcangelo's realized that I'm not going to go through with becoming an assassin so he has to solve the problem the only way he can think of."

"Which is to kill you,"

"Exactly," Ezio said, pacing back and forth, another theory forming in his mind. "But maybe he's not going to kill me. Not yet, anyway."

"What do you mean?"

"He might be trying to scare me. I'm still the guy they want. I'm still the guy that will 'ignite the spark' in the other assassins. Arcangelo might be just trying to scare me into giving up and saying okay to becoming an assassin. And what's the best way to scare me?'"

"To almost burn you to death?" Marco replied. Ezio shook his head.

"Arcangelo knows I'd rather die—as much as that would suck—than become an assassin," he explained. "The way he's going to scare me is to threaten you guys. He's going to threaten your lives to get to me. If I think you and dad and Santos are going to die, then I'll give in to save the three of you."

"He's not actually going to kill us, is he?" Marco asked, his voice quiet. Ezio glanced over at him.

"It's a dangerous game we're playing. If he threatens to kill you, I could give in right away, or I could call his bluff. If he actually kills you, I could resolve that I have nothing left and join the assassins, or I could go on a rampage and kill everyone in the Order. He doesn't know what's going on inside my head. He won't know if he's pushed too far."

"So it's all a guessing game with him?"

"Basically, yeah." Marco thought it over and nodded.

"So if you're expendable, then why doesn't he just accept the fact you're saying no?"

"Because they need a replacement before they can let me go. They need to be absolutely sure they've got the next leader."

"The leader or the scapegoat?"

"They'd prefer to have an actual leader who wants the same thing they want. But they'd be fine with a scapegoat." Ezio crossed over to the door and felt it. It was burning hot to the touch, and he swore the wood was flexing under the heat.

"Okay, we've got to find a way out of here. Preferably a way up to the first floor."

"What's that?" Marco asked, pointing to a small crawl space on the floor near the far wall. Ezio crouched down and looked through the rectangular hole. No fire. That was good.

"Let's try it."

The hole was big enough for the boys to fit through if they slid on their bellies. Ezio went first, and Marco followed. They were in another corridor, this one still without windows. Ezio assumed they were still underground. Stalactites hung from the ceilings, but when Ezio tasted the droplets that were dripping down to the floor, they didn't taste like the vile kerosene in the other tunnel system.

"I think we're okay,"[1]

They walked around a corner and came across a set of over a dozen steps, which were wide and elegant. They were made out of a white stone of some sort, perhaps marble, and there were torches guiding

114

the boys' way up. Marco and Ezio ascended the stairs without hesitation.

"Now we just need to find dad and Santos," Marco said as he took one of the torches off the wall and held it before them.

"Whoa," Ezio muttered. They were in a large room with high arched ceilings, and against a far wall was a ten-foot tall crucifix. It was something Ezio would have expected to find at the Vatican—not in the castle of a killer. The light from the torches didn't extend all the way to the crucifix, but Ezio could make out the general shape. It was eerie and made his skin crawl. The crucifix he saw at church every Sunday wasn't nearly as big as this one. This was like something out of Rio de Janeiro.

"This is creepy," Marco whispered, as if people were listening to them and would be hurt if they heard he didn't like the décor. Ezio pointed next to the crucifix.

"Is that a hallway?" he asked. Marco nodded.

"Let's get out of here."

The hall led to yet another set of stairs, this one unlit, but at the very top of the narrow, steep staircase was a rectangle of light. This one wasn't moving. It was a doorway lit by not a ravaging fire, but a lamp.

"Think that's it?" Marco asked. Ezio didn't say anything. He didn't want to jinx it.

It was, indeed, 'it.' The boys emerged from the stairwell, faces and clothes black with soot, into the foyer of the castle.

"Thank God," Marco muttered tiredly. They had escaped from the tunnels with their lives, but this was far from over.

"You psycho *asino!*" the unmistakable voice of Tony Ferrari shouted somewhere nearby. "You stay away from my sons!" Then there was a gunshot.

"Did dad bring a gun?" Ezio asked frantically, remembering the small pistol Tony kept in a box on the top shelf of his closet. He hoped his dad *had* brought the firearm; he didn't care to think about what would happen if Arcangelo had more than just daggers.

"Yeah, he said it was 'just in case.'" Marco replied.

Ezio took off in a dead sprint despite being exhausted from his second run-in with fire. Marco lagged behind but kept up at a good pace. The gunshot had come from their dad's gun, but that didn't mean Arcangelo hadn't escalated things and taken the weapon from him. *And who knows where Santos is.*

They found Tony chasing after Arcangelo, running up the winding staircase. They joined him, after grabbing their coats and the book, and made sure he was aware of their presence so he didn't shoot them accidentally.

"What happened to you guys?" he asked as they chased the assassin up the stairs. His sons were covered in soot from head to toe; they looked like they had just swept a few chimneys.

"Long story. Have you seen Santos?"

"I was looking for him when I ran across this dirtbag," Tony said. "He told me you two were gonna die."

"Well, we were. But we got out of it." Marco answered. "He kind of lit us on fire."

"More of a reason to shoot the *asino*!" Tony spat. He obviously liked the term *asino*. He aimed the gun at Arcangelo and fired again. The bullet sailed through the air and lodged in the wall Arcangelo had just crossed in front of.

"Dad, you suck at shooting," Marco said. Tony looked at his son.

"I'm sorry, this is real life, not a video game. I don't have aim-assist here." Marco's face grew red.

"Can we please focus on finding Santos?" Ezio asked. "This is fun and all, but I'm not sure how we're going to explain it to Mrs. Ogechi if her son gets *killed*."

"Right," Tony agreed.

"Did you try calling him?" Marco asked. Ezio stopped dead in his tracks.

"Good idea," he said, dumbfounded he hadn't thought of that earlier.

He took out his cell phone and quickly dialed Santos' number. It rang a few times before he heard a familiar voice.

"Took you long enough, I've been trying to call you for like, fifteen minutes."

"We were kind of busy. Sorry. Where are you?"

"On the third floor, hiding in a library. Where are you guys?"

"Second floor. We're on our way, hang tight."

"There's nothing else I can really do." Ezio hung up and slipped his phone back in his pocket.

"He's on the third floor. Dad—" Tony was about to go after Arcangelo. "—forget about him. Let's just get out of here."

Reluctantly, Tony followed his sons up the stairs to the third floor. They walked down the red velvet carpet, putting their coats on as they passed torches and more malevolent-faced paintings of past Hône Order leaders. Ezio couldn't imagine living in a castle where dozens of paintings such as these hung on the walls, staring at you, watching your every move as you passed by. But then again, if he lived here, that would mean he was an assassin like Arcangelo. Which in turn meant that he would probably be at a point where he felt nothing. No fear. No remorse. He probably wouldn't even feel joy, unless he was killing someone.

That's actually really sad, Ezio thought as he hurried down the hall. *These assassins don't feel joy unless they're murdering someone. How can anyone live like that?* Then Ezio realized: some people can't. Renato, Bernardo, Angelo, Arcadia, and Matteo couldn't. That's why the left the Order and formed their rebel group. *That's why they're trying to help me. Because they know I can't live like they did.*

It hadn't been an insult when Angelo called Ezio sensitive over the summer. It had been a statement to protect him. It just meant Ezio wouldn't be capable of killing without feeling. And that wasn't necessarily a bad thing. Sure, it had ruined his plan of killing Arcangelo, but at the same time, he *hadn't killed Arcangelo.* He hadn't given in. He hadn't committed murder, not even in self-defense. *I'm still me,* he thought. He felt a little glimmer of hope. *I can get out of this.*

The library was in the middle of a corridor that branched off the main one; it overlooked the plateau formed by the hill. The door was shut and locked from the inside — Santos was taking precautions.

"Santos, open up, it's us," Ezio said as he knocked on the door. There was a click as the lock was undone, and the knob turned to allow Santos' relieved face to fill the doorway. "Can we go now? Please?" was the first thing he said. And then, after Ezio and Marco's appearances registered, it was, "Dude, what happened?"

"Long story," Ezio gave the same reply to Santos as he did to his dad. "Here's your coat." He handed his friend his borrowed coat and glanced around. "Where do you think Arcangelo is?"

"I don't know but I don't want to find out," Marco said. "He kind of wants to kill us."

"Well that much is obvious," Tony muttered.

Ezio walked into the library, wondering if maybe there were more things in here that could be useful, like the book he was carrying. Santos and Marco followed, looking with him.

"What's the book for?" Santos asked, nodding to the record tucked under one of Ezio's arms.

"It's like a history book, only it's just on the Order," Ezio replied.

"And it's not yours," a voice drawled from the doorway. Ezio, Marco, and Santos turned around and saw *Arcangelo Della Morte* standing before them, a knife held closely to Tony's neck. "Put the book down, Ezio."

Ezio did as he was told and set the book down on the desk that stood in the middle of the room. Tony looked more angry than scared as the knife pressed against his skin. Behind him, using him as a shield, stood Arcangelo. He was pale, almost ghostly looking, and talked with a mixed accent of Italian and French. He was in his early sixties, with dark grey hair and thin, light pink lips. He was dressed in a black, pressed, button-up shirt and black trousers. He had black eyes that danced menacingly in the torch light. Everything about him radiated death. The aura of an assassin.

"Now, I think you've figured out by now what I want," Arcangelo said.

"I'm not going to be an assassin," Ezio replied in anticipation.

"Then I guess you're going to be fatherless." Ezio smirked. He had been right. Arcangelo was bluffing, even if he didn't look it. The assassin pressed the blade into Tony's neck, and a drop of blood appeared. Tony didn't move, but his eyes did shut.

"You're not going to do it," Ezio said, taking a step forward. "Because you know that if you kill any of my friends or my family, I will take down you and the Hône Order on my own. I will destroy you." Arcangelo tut-tutted at him.

"Not if you're dead too,"

"Then you won't have your scapegoat," Ezio said, pretending he didn't already know he was expendable.

"Don't you understand, Ezio? You are disposable. We don't *need* you. What matters is the name, the skills, and the generation you're a part of. We can find another boy and call him Ezio, and train him to be just as good as you would be. It will take a little more work, but it's a good thing I don't shy away from a challenge. Italy will be taken down one way or another, with or without you. I can kill everyone in this room and my plan will go on unhindered." Ezio took another step forward. Arcangelo tightened his grip on his father, but they both knew he wouldn't do anything. He could not take that risk.

With a small smirk still on his face, Ezio said in a low, challenging voice, daring the man:

EXPENDABLE

"Do it."

CHAPTER THIRTEEN
ESCAPE

For a long time, Arcangelo and Ezio stared at each other. Ezio was daring him, and Arcangelo wasn't ready to stop bluffing. If Ezio doubted his confidence in calling Arcangelo's bluff, he never showed it. Finally, Arcangelo released Tony and shoved him into the library.

"Just wait," he muttered. "I will ruin your life."

"You already have," Ezio countered. "You seem to be good at that."

"You know of my work?" Arcangelo asked with a sly grin.

"I know you killed Bernardo Moretti." The assassin stiffened.

"He was a traitor," he hissed. "He deserved it."

"He deserved to be stabbed in the neck? He deserved to be burned to ashes?"

"He deserved it all," Arcangelo said, raising his voice. "He was a traitor against the people who made him who he was —"

"An assassin? He didn't want to be a killer. Strange how that theme seems to be repeating itself, huh?" Arcangelo glared at Ezio.

"You don't know anything,"

"I do know Bernardo and Angelo—"

"Enough with Bernardo," Arcangelo muttered. "He made the wrong decision, and he paid for it. Just like when we were kids. Some things never change." Ezio glanced over at Santos, whose eyebrows were raised in shock. Arcangelo and Bernardo grew up together? Did that mean they were—

"Bernardo was your older brother," Ezio said, putting the pieces together. Arcangelo raised his gaze to meet Ezio's with an ominous glare.

"*Half* brother," he corrected the boy. "And a terrible one, at that."

"How could you kill your own brother?" Ezio asked. He couldn't imagine killing Marco or Milan, under any circumstance.

"Because he was a traitor," Arcangelo replied simply, as if that made the crime perfectly acceptable.

"Just like Angelo."

"And me," Ezio said. "If I become an assassin, you can be sure I won't work with you."

"You'll do as I want," Arcangelo said. "When your family and all of your friends die, you won't have anyone or anything to go back to. There will be no reason for you to rebel."

Before anyone had time to react, Arcangelo slammed the library door shut. Ezio dove for it, trying to turn the knob before Arcangelo had a chance to lock it. But the assassin was too quick.

"Do the knife thing again," Marco said eagerly, his eyes hopeful his brother would get them out of this situation, too. "Pick the lock." Ezio tried. He tried for ten minutes, to no avail.

"Why would he do this?" Tony asked when Ezio finally gave up. "Why does he want to keep us here?"

"Because," Ezio said, sitting down on the ground and leaning against the door. "If I'm stuck here I won't have any other choice but to become an assassin."

"You said he can make you an assassin any time he wants, right?" Santos asked. "So why not just take you now and let us go? No offense." Ezio grinned.

"None taken. But I guess he just really hates me or something. I mean, I did just call his bluff."

"Speaking of which," Tony said, rubbing his neck at the memory of the knife pressed up against it. There was a thin red line from where the blade had been. "How did you know that was a bluff?"

"Me and Marco talked about it earlier. We figured Arcangelo was going to threaten you guys to get to me."

"Well I'm glad that guy's predictable," Tony muttered. He would have sacrificed himself for his son like any parent would, but when there was a knife pressed to your throat, you kind of second guess yourself for an instant.

"So now what do we do?" Marco asked. They all turned to Ezio for an answer. But Ezio was out of answers. He was tired. He wanted to go home.

"I don't know," he said. "I guess we just sit here."

"What?" Marco asked. "You just saved us from getting burned to a crisp. You pulled a dagger out of my shoulder. You always know what to do."

"We're stuck in here. There aren't any vents to crawl through. If you want to jump out the window, go right ahead. It's a long way down, though." Tony, Marco, and Santos stared at Ezio. He was just giving up. It was like he didn't want to fight anymore. It was like he didn't care.

Santos walked over to the window and looked outside. There was deep snow below, but they were twenty feet up, give or take. It seemed too far to jump without getting hurt.

"Look, Ezio, you can give up and stay here, but we aren't. I'd rather not die or spend the rest of my life in

Hône. No offense, but I kind of want to get back to my family." Santos said.

"I know, I get that. I want to go home too. But right now I can't come up with anything. I just need time to think."

For two hours they sat in the library, not really talking. Ezio ripped off part of his shirt again to change the dressing on Marco's injury. Tony took his gun apart, then put it back together. Santos sat cross-legged on the floor and fiddled with the aglet on the end of his shoe lace.

Finally, after what felt like an eternity, there was a click and the door knob began to turn. Ezio stood up and pressed the button on the brace beneath his coat sleeve. He made up his mind. He would kill Arcangelo, without any hesitation, no matter how awful it may be.

The door swung open and Ezio lunged forward, ready to jab the blade up into Arcangelo's chest. But someone grabbed his wrist to stop him. Ezio looked up.

"You're the man from the Palazzo," he said in disbelief.

"Arcadia Conti, at your service. Now, if you'd please come with me, we need to get out of here."

Ezio took a step forward to follow Arcadia, a little surprised to find he trusted the assassin, but his dad put a hand on his shoulder.

"Do you know this guy?" he asked. Ezio glanced at Arcadia, then nodded.

"Yeah," he replied. "I saved his life."

"Come on, all of you," Arcadia urgently intervened. "We need to get out before Arcangelo realizes I'm—"

"Here? Hello, Arcadia."

Standing at the end of the hallway was Arcangelo, in all his pale glory. He seemed amused Arcadia was in the castle. Ezio noticed his hand was behind his back —he had a dagger.

"Arcangelo," Arcadia nodded in greeting. He put his arm out to push Ezio, Tony, Marco, and Santos back into the library. The others moved, but Ezio stayed where he was.

"What a pleasant surprise," Arcangelo intoned. "How is your nephew? I was planning on killing him next, saving Angelo for last. I'm sorry you were going to be the first to go—but I thought it fitting you'd be killed at the Palazzo, in front of your politician brother who has no idea you work for me."

"I don't work for you," Arcadia replied, again trying to push Ezio back. Instead, Ezio took a step forward. Arcadia shot him a sideways look that the teen ignored.

"Does Aurelio know you allowed his son to become an assassin?" Arcangelo asked in a taunting voice. The younger assassin's jaw tightened, but other than that, he did not react.

"Ezio, go back into the library," Arcadia muttered. Ezio didn't move. Arcadia turned his head slightly, but kept his eyes on Arcangelo. "Now."

Tony pulled Ezio into the library. He had missed his chance, his third chance, to kill Arcangelo. Now it was up to Arcadia to deal with him.

Arcadia pushed the library door shut and began talking to Arcangelo. Ezio tried to listen, but the two were talking quietly.

"Now what?" Marco asked. "Do we just wait here or something?" Ezio pressed his ear to the door, struggling to hear the conversation. Suddenly, he heard what sounded like a scuffle.

"They're fighting," he told the others, a little excited. Maybe Arcadia would kill Arcangelo for him. Then this would all be over.

"Ezio, run!" Arcadia shouted.

"Why?" Ezio asked, even though Arcadia couldn't hear him. He heard something fall to the ground, and the fighting continued. Ezio turned to the others. There were two ways out of the library: through the hall, where Arcadia and Arcangelo were fighting, or through the window. They all knew which option was the more plausible—though not the most logical.

"Try to tuck and roll," Ezio advised. "The snow should be pretty deep so that might cushion our fall."

"'Might?'" Santos asked. "What do you mean 'might?'" Ezio shrugged.

"Well I can't be sure, now can I?"

"So we're supposed to just blindly jump down there?"

"Don't forget to tuck and roll," Santos looked at him.

"You're not serious are you?"

A slew of curse words and punches from outside the library erupted, and gave Santos his answer. Ezio crossed over to the window and pushed it open.

"Who wants to go first?"

CHAPTER FOURTEEN
HE FORGOT TO TUCK AND ROLL

Marco went first, and landed successfully. He rolled when he landed, snow billowing up around the point of impact. Ezio, Tony, and Santos watched anxiously to see if Marco would get up. After a moment, he did.

"That was awesome!" Marco shouted up to them as he backed away from the window to a safe distance. From twenty feet up, they could tell he was grinning.

"Dad? Santos? Which one of you wants to go next?"

"You go, Mr. Ferrari," Santos said, taking a step away from the window.

"You sure?" Tony asked, peering down at the ground uncomfortably.

"I've never been so sure in my life," Santos muttered.

"Alright then," Tony said quietly, climbing onto the window sill. "I think I'm a little old for this stuff, but I guess I've got no choice."

He jumped from the window, his legs bent in a crouching position, and landed a few inches from where Marco had. He got up immediately, and joined Marco near the edge of the hill. Ezio and Santos looked at each other.

"You first," Ezio said. "I'll be right behind you." Santos looked at him, knowing his friend wasn't telling the truth.

"Be careful, Ezio," he told him. "You don't need to get involved."

"I'll be fine," Ezio replied. "Be careful jumping."

Santos nodded and went to the window. He climbed up, looked down, and took a deep breath. *This is a terrible idea*, he thought to himself. He leaned himself forward, not sure if he would actually be able to let go of the wall.

Someone kicked in the library door, startling Santos. He shouted and lost his footing on the icy window sill, and began falling to the ground. Ezio didn't have time to watch his friend land; he was too busy watching the man in the doorway.

A bloody and bruised Arcadia Conti stood, breathing heavily, pointing down the hallway.

"That guy," he said, his voice raspy. "Does not want to die."

"What's going on?" Ezio asked.

"He ran away like a little girl. Come on, we need to get out of here. He'll come back." Ezio grabbed the book off the desk and headed toward the window. He climbed onto the sill and hesitated for a brief moment. It was a long way down, but why should he worry? The others had landed without a problem, why would this time be any different?

Ezio hadn't accounted for the fact the snow had been displaced by the other three bodies that had landed close together. The snow level was lower than it had been before Marco had jumped, so Ezio's landing was harder. His bones rattled in his body, and his side was bruised from landing on the solid, frozen ground.

"Are you okay?" Tony asked, helping his son up. Ezio nodded.

"Are you guys?"

"Yeah, Santos sprained his ankle but I think he's okay." Ezio looked over at Santos, who was leaning against Marco.

"He forgot to tuck and roll," Marco explained. "He kind of just...flopped."

Arcadia landed behind Ezio with graceful expertise. He stood up and brushed the snow off his jacket.

"Where are you guys staying?" he asked, not wanting them to know he had been watching them in the lobby of their hotel. Marco hadn't recognized him, so why reveal it? Arcadia thought it was kind of fun to keep the ploy up.

"At a hotel over on Via Lecco," Ezio replied. He didn't know the name; it had seemed like such a minor detail compared to the task at hand.

"You can't stay there," Arcadia muttered, starting down the hill. "He'll find you. You need to get out of Hône."

"Right now?" Tony asked. "It's almost one o'clock in the morning."

"I know,"

"And it's snowing," Tony said. For the first time, Ezio realized fat snowflakes were falling from the sky; he had been so focused on getting everyone out of the castle he hadn't noticed.

"If you don't want to drive all the way to Rome, you can go to Verona," Arcadia suggested. "Angelo's got a fortified compound on the outskirts of town." Tony glanced down at the ground at the mention of Angelo Lombardi, the uncle that he believed was dead. The man who forced him into signing Ezio's life away.

"We have to leave right now?" he asked again.

"I would strongly advise it," Arcadia answered. "Marco, Santos, hurry up please."

"Doing the best we can," Marco replied, his voice strained from holding Santos up. He was helping him down the hill, trying to keep him from falling.

They made good time down to the parking lot where they had left the car. They quickly climbed in, including Arcadia, who sat in the back seat next to Santos.

"Did you leave anything at the hotel?" he asked. Tony shook his head.

"All the suitcases are in the trunk, but don't you think we should check out—"

"No," Arcadia answered gruffly. "If you paid in cash you're fine."

Tony started the car and began driving. As they began to leave Hône, the weather grew worse, turning into a blizzard once again. They took their time and didn't let their guard down until they got to the border of Aosta Valley.

It was a three hour drive to Verona in the blizzard, despite there not being many other cars on the road. Santos and Marco fell asleep after about an hour; Ezio found it impossible to even doze off.

"What exactly happened back there?" Tony asked as they pulled into the sleeping city. The headlights danced ahead of them on the road, casting light on the sidewalks and deserted buildings.

"Arcangelo's not dead," Arcadia replied tiredly. "But he's hurt. He'll be out of commission for a while."

"He's not going to come after my son?" Tony asked, oblivious to the fact Ezio was still awake.

"He might," Arcadia sighed. "But I think Ezio can take care of himself. He managed to stay alive today, and he's paranoid enough as it is, so I don't think you need to worry."

"And the rest of my family? My wife, my other kids? Ezio's friends?"

"Arcangelo won't do anything to them. Ezio already called his bluff. He knows he can't play that card anymore."

"What happens when March 14 comes around?"

"The assassins will take him to a secret training facility. It used to be in Hône, but since the rebel group was formed, three other locations, maybe more, have popped up. I know there are three in other parts of Europe, but I don't know their exact locations. Ezio could be taken to any one of those, plus any one of the others I don't know about."

"So basically if the assassins get their hands on Ezio, we'll never see him again?"

"Correct,"

"He wouldn't be able to leave?"

"It would be difficult. He'd be a prisoner wherever he was held. I know Ezio would have little to no trouble getting out of whatever situation he was thrown into, but the assassins are aware of that as well. The security detail on him would be tighter than the one on the Prime Minister."

There was silence in the car for a few minutes as they drove through the town. When Tony neared Viale Machiavelli, the road that Angelo Lombardi had built his compound on, Arcadia told him to turn left. Ezio recognized the dirt road and the open fields, and remembered how long it had taken him and his friends to walk to the compound. He remembered the field they slept in, and the bright spotlights and the alarm that made maneuvering through the compound almost unbearable. He could feel the daggers whiz past him as if Angelo was throwing them right there in the car—that now seemed to be an assassin's go-to tactic when dealing with him. Ezio thought he would never return to Angelo's compound, especially after finding out the hit on his uncle Sam had been fake, and that everything he and his friends had gone through was a test. Yet, here he was.

It was hard to miss the compound, even at night. Arcadia had Tony stop by the gate, and he got out to punch a number into the control panel that was mounted on the concrete wall. The gate buzzed and began opening; Arcadia gave Tony the okay to drive through.

"I'm going to go in the house so he doesn't kill us," Arcadia said casually as he crouched to be level with the driver's side window. "Park next to the garage and come inside."

Arcadia walked briskly down the off-white concrete driveway to the house. Ezio watched as he opened the unlocked door and disappeared inside. Angelo still wasn't locking his front door. *With Arcangelo wanting him dead, you'd think he'd take more precautions.*

"Wake up," Tony said, shaking Marco awake gently. "We're here." Ezio elbowed Santos, whose eyes shot open. He glanced out the window and recognized where they were.

"Great," he said quietly. "This guy again."

"Is this Angelo's place?" Marco asked Ezio. He nodded, and Marco sighed. "It'll be weird seeing a dead guy."

CHAPTER FIFTEEN
DEAD MAN WALKING

Tony stared with a mixture of confoundedness and disgust at the old rambling man standing three feet away. He was supposed to be in a coffin six feet under the ground in Rome, yet he was standing in front of them in Verona, making sandwiches for the hungry travelers. Angelo didn't notice his nephew's discomfort; he wasn't the type to pay attention to other people's feelings.

"It's quite funny that Arcangelo didn't kill you," he was saying nonchalantly to Arcadia. "It almost makes you think he's dropped the ball. As if he's too *old* for this stuff." Angelo chuckled at the joke only he understood, and handed Tony a paper plate with a sandwich on it.

"He came pretty close," Arcadia muttered as he took off his jacket for the first time. "Came way too close to an artery." Ezio noticed the black shirt Arcadia had on underneath the jacket was torn in one place, and the fabric surrounding the tear was wet with blood. He had been stabbed in the chest, but didn't seem too worried about it. Marco stared at the man in awe—he had gotten a dagger stuck in his shoulder and thought he was going to die. Arcadia was acting as if nothing happened.

"Well did you at least get him back?" Angelo asked as he prepared Marco's sandwich next. Santos and Ezio had declined food; neither of them were very hungry after the night's events.

"Of course," Arcadia replied, as if the idea of him not stabbing Arcangelo was absurd. "Stabbed him in the chest too. Don't know if it was serious or not, since he walked away and I was in a rush, but I hope it was."

"Don't we all," Angelo muttered. "How's Matteo doing?"

"Still watching the house," Arcadia replied. "I'm going to have him move soon, though. Now that Arcangelo knows for sure we're helping Ezio, he's bound to go after all three of us at once. I need him to be secure."

"What house?" Tony asked. "Is someone watching our house?" Arcadia and Angelo looked at each other.

"Yes, my nephew, Matteo, is renting the house across from yours. Don't worry, no other assassins know he's there. Your wife and daughters are perfectly safe." Arcadia replied, covering all the bases before Tony had time to freak out. He nodded, and there was silence. No one knew what to talk about. Ezio had a lot of questions, but he felt like those could wait.

"Why did you do it?" Tony finally asked. It was random, and no one was sure what he was talking about at first.

"Do what?" Angelo asked.

"Fake your own death. Why'd you do it?"

"The CIA was onto me," Angelo told him apathetically. He never took into consideration that people *actually* thought him dead—he was egocentric and believed that if *he* knew he had been alive all this time, then everyone else had to. Well, everyone but the police and all of those pesky government agencies. "I needed to disappear. The best way to do that was to fake my death."

"But you put our family through unnecessary grief. You couldn't have just disappeared without any explanation? I mean, that wouldn't have been much better, but at least my mother wouldn't have—"

"Your mother knew I was still alive," Angelo interrupted. "I figured you and Sam wouldn't have cared if I was dead or missing; I would have been out of your lives." Tony glanced down at his hands, drawing Angelo's attention to them.

"You took the ring off," he observed. Tony looked up.

"Of course I did," he snapped. "It was the ring of the organization that wants to take my son away."

"Understandable," Angelo muttered, nodding. But it was evident he was a little hurt. Despite his hatred of Arcangelo, the Hône Order of Assassins had once been his own. He had dedicated his life to it. He loved it.

"So...what's our next move?" Ezio asked, trying to alleviate some of the tension in the room by changing the subject.

"There are two options," Arcadia replied. "The first option is to go to Alaska and live the rest of your life in limited contact with the rest of the world, or, you stay in Italy and fight off the 200+ assassins who will be coming after you in less than a year."

"I'm guessing you want me to fight them?"

"Well, it'd be more definite than just running away," Ezio sighed. He was hoping there would be another way to solve this.

"What do you mean by 'fight?'"

"Kill them," Angelo said bluntly. "After you get through a dozen assassins, the others will scatter."

"In case you haven't noticed, Angelo, the kid's kind of, you know...not into the whole killing thing." Arcadia said as if Ezio couldn't hear him.

"I'm aware,"

"Matteo and I could help him, but at the moment I think our best bet is to send him to Lampedusa."

"Lampedusa?" Ezio asked. "Where's that?"

"South of Sicily, about seventy miles from Tunisia," Arcadia answered. "It's a small island with a lot of North African immigrants. We have contacts down there and a safe house. It would be better than Alaska, but it'd be temporary. Maybe just for a month or two, until we can figure out a more definite plan."

"He's not going to Lampedusa," Tony said. "How would we explain that to his mother?"

"We wouldn't," Arcadia said coolly. "You would." Tony glared at the assassin, who held his gaze. Arcadia didn't really care for Tony. The man was too overprotective of the son he had agreed to send away. Granted, Tony regretted the decision now, but what man does that in the first place?

"If you don't go to Lampedusa, there's a greater chance of Arcangelo kidnapping you before your birthday. Honestly, you should just get off the mainland so that no one finds you. Ever. At midnight..." Angelo's voice trailed off when he saw the dirty look Arcadia was giving him.

"I thought we agreed we wouldn't tell him about that."

"Tell me what?" Ezio asked. Arcadia ignored him, and Angelo hurriedly stood up.

"Santos, can I get you anything for your leg? More ice?"

"No thanks," Santos replied. He had a bundle of ice in a towel already held to his sprained ankle, and his leg was propped up on a chair.

"Tell me what?" Ezio asked again. "What happens at midnight?" Arcadia and Angelo looked at each other, and reluctantly, Arcadia shrugged.

"The assassins have until 11:59 p.m. on March 14, 2015 to make you one of them," Angelo answered. "At 12:00 a.m. on March 15, they have free reign to kill you for noncompliance."

CHAPTER SIXTEEN
GAME CHANGER

"That's not part of the deal!" Tony shouted at Angelo. "You never said anything about him dying!" His shouts were met with a steely glare as they ricocheted off the old man. They held no meaning for him.

Silence enveloped the kitchen. Tony's shouts died out, and it was as though he had spoken into a void. No one seemed to be effected by his protests, not even Ezio. The teenager was just sitting there, frozen, eyes locked on Angelo. Everyone stared at him, waiting anxiously to see his reaction.

"This changes everything," he finally whispered. His eyes moved over to Arcadia. "Why didn't you tell me?"

"I didn't think you needed to know right away," he replied quietly. "I thought you could take Arcangelo down before your birthday and you'd never need to know about the hit."

"Hold on a second," Marco said angrily. "You mean you *knew?* We were just in a car with you for three hours after almost getting stabbed and burned to death, and you never thought to mention that my brother will be killed the day after his sixteenth birthday? Glad to know where your priorities are at. All of you people are insane."

The "insane" comment referred not only to the assassins in the room, but also Tony, whether Marco intended it or not. His remark wounded his father, who looked up at his eldest child, the hurt evident in his eyes. Marco did not notice, though; his attention had been redirected to Ezio, who was opening his mouth to speak again.

"I get why you didn't tell me," he said slowly, thinking carefully before he spoke. "But this changes the entire situation. It would have helped to know that if I don't do what Arcangelo wants, I'll be killed. Any plans we make have to be adjusted to include that, right? What am I supposed to do now?"

"Kill Arcangelo before he kills you," Angelo mumbled as though the idea was simple and obvious.

"Shut up," Arcadia muttered to him, not caring if Angelo was his superior not only in rank, but also in skill. He turned back to Ezio. "We'll figure it out. We have plenty of time, as long as everything goes our way. And we'll make sure it does."

"But what's our next step?" Santos asked, not settling for Arcadia's beat-around-the-bush response. "Ezio's right—this changes everything. Any plan we could have hoped to have before this kind of goes out the window. Even if he was to leave and go to Lampedusa, what's to stop the assassins from killing him?"

"Nothing, really," Angelo replied before Arcadia could get in a word. "Which is why Arcangelo's death is so necessary."

Silence once again took over the room, and a rushing sound began to fill Ezio's ears. He felt sick to his stomach. He had to get out of here. He pushed his chair back, stumbling away from it so clumsily that it crashed to the floor.

"Ezio, where are you—" He wasn't sure who said it, but he wasn't going to stick around to find out. He bolted out of the room, his chest feeling as tight as it did when Bernardo's hut was burning to the ground. He blindly ran through the hallway and pulled open the front door. The cold winter air felt like a slap to the face as it surged into the house, but it didn't bother him. He ran out into the darkness, knowing for the first time in several hours exactly where he was going.

*   *   *   *   *   *

It was a cold, miserable night. Snow covered the fields around Angelo Lombardi's compound. The trees were bare, the plants were dead, and the grass beneath the snow was brown and wet. Ezio had cleared away the snow beneath a large olive tree in the field across from the compound, and was now sitting there with his back to it. It was the same tree that he and his friends had hidden behind when a mysterious car was driving down Viale Machiavelli. It turned out the car was just delivering Luke to rejoin the mission to stop Angelo, but at the time, they thought it was an assassin. *How was a tree going to protect us?* Ezio wondered as he leaned back against it, turning his head up towards the sky. The moon was barely visible behind the clouds that night. It was just a faded patch of glowing yellow behind the dark, ambiguous shapes that came as a package deal with storms.

Ezio didn't mind the cold, although he was a bit concerned about getting sick. That was, of course, after the nausea had passed and he no longer had to worry about keeping his dinner down. He had somehow managed to calm himself and end the panic he felt in the kitchen. Being alone helped; there were too many people in the kitchen, with too much information for him to process comfortably.

No one had come looking for him yet, which he was grateful for. He needed the isolation. This kind of silence was not intolerable. In fact, it was welcome. There wasn't anyone staring at him out here. No one waiting for him to speak. He could breathe easy out here, and that's exactly what he did. One deep breath after another, reminding himself that he wasn't dead and wasn't going to be. He had people helping him. He was alone out here, but not in his fight against the Hône Order of Assassins.

Eventually, he would have to go back inside. He would have to face reality and return to Rome, put on a front for his mother and sisters, and all of his classmates at school, and go on with his life. All with the knowledge that there would be a bounty on his head if he didn't become an assassin. The thought brought the panic back, but he suppressed it, closing his eyes and telling himself he didn't have to go back inside just yet. He had time.

He could have easily fallen asleep beneath the olive tree, and probably slept for seven hours straight, if it wasn't for the sound of footsteps coming from the other side of the road. He didn't move or open his eyes, because he had a feeling of who it was.

The source of the footsteps made it to the tree, stopped, saw he was there, and sat down in a snowless patch. He didn't say anything to Ezio at first. He enjoyed the silence, too.

"They're bickering like a bunch of twelve-year-olds in there," his new companion finally said. "Milan would cringe at the insults they're using." Ezio could sense Santos rolling his eyes in the darkness.

"Is that why you came out here?" he asked.

"Yeah, that and I was worried you might get frostbite." Both boys smirked at that; back in June, Luke had been concerned about developing frostbite during their night in this field. It took a while for Santos to convince him that would not happen—Luke wasn't always the most reasonable person.

"Don't worry about me, I'm all good. Sort of, anyway." Even though Ezio couldn't see him, Santos nodded understandingly.

"I know this is tough. It was tough before, but now that the stakes are higher, it feels one hundred times more difficult. I'm sorry."

"For what?" Ezio asked, opening his eyes. "You didn't start any of this. You didn't promise Arcangelo anything. You weren't the one who decided I would die if I didn't become an assassin."

"I know, but it just sucks. You're fighting an uphill battle against an army that's twenty times bigger than ours. We can't even consider ourselves an army. If we were in the military, we'd be a squad."

"If we were in the military we'd have a better chance," Ezio muttered bitterly. Santos paused.

"We do have a chance, though," he said softly.

"How? I don't have many options that will work in my favor. If I kill Arcangelo...I can't even imagine killing someone, Santos. I don't know what I expected to achieve tonight. I don't know what I would have done if I really killed that guy. I think I might just be better off giving myself up to the Order. Maybe I'll find a way to escape, to make it back home afterwards —"

"No," Santos said sternly, turning to face his friend. "You are not giving yourself up. You've come way to far to just give it all away. You cheated death twice this weekend, so damn it, Ezio, you're not going down without a fight. You have too much going for you in this life to just throw it away."

"What do you mean?"

"Football? Or soccer, whatever the hell you call it nowadays? You're good enough to go pro. And you're smart enough to get a scholarship to a really good university and make something of yourself. You're just going to give up your education, your sport, your life, so you don't have to worry about getting murdered? Well, if that's the case, board up your house and never leave, because you're alive. And if you're alive, you can be killed. Just because the odds of you being killed have increased, doesn't mean it's going to happen. I'm not going to sit by and watch you wallow in self-pity and give up. That's not the Ezio I know. The Ezio I know would stand up and fight. You do it on the field all the time, so why can't you do it now? Last season we were down 0-3 against San Michele and we ended up beating them 4-3 in the second half. Everybody said we had no chance, there was no way to come back from that deficit. But somehow, we pulled it off, and we went on to win the national championship two weeks later. This isn't much different. The assassins don't think we have a chance. We're outmatched. We are the underdogs here. But I have faith we will win."

Ezio grinned. This was why Santos was one of his best friends. He was level-headed when his emotions got the best of him, logical when he was irrational. And, he knew how to give a pep talk.

"You're right," he said, standing up and brushing the grass off of his pants. "We do have a shot. It might be the worst shot in history, but at least it's something." Santos chuckled and climbed to his feet.

"That's the spirit. Come on, let's go back inside. It's freezing out here."

Feeling better than when he first came outside, Ezio happily walked alongside his friend as they returned to the compound. Though he was uncertain as to what the future held for him, he knew one thing for sure: he would not go down without a fight.

CHAPTER SEVENTEEN
UP TO SPEED

"Do you think they're alright?" Giovanni asked as the three of them sat around in Luke's bedroom. It was four o'clock in the morning and none of them had heard from Ezio or Santos since they left for Hône. They had no way of knowing if they needed help, or if they were even alive.

"I'm sure they're fine," Milan answered distractedly.

"Yeah, Ezio can take care of himself," Luke added, knowing how worried Milan was about his brothers. "They'll probably call soon."

None of them had slept that night. Each of them had their phones nearby, waiting and hoping for a call from one of their friends to give them an update. At six o'clock, when the three were finally beginning to doze off in spite of themselves, Milan's cell phone rang loudly. Their eyes snapped open, startled by the sudden sound, and Milan scrambled for his phone. He answered and put the call on speaker phone, with the volume only loud enough so Luke and Giovanni could hear.

"Hey, are you guys okay?" he asked quietly, so not to wake up the rest of Luke's family.

"Yeah, we're fine. A little bruised, but nothing major. We're in Verona right now," Ezio replied. He didn't want to tell his friends about the new information he had learned just yet.

"At Angelo's compound?" Giovanni guessed. It was the only place in the town he was really familiar with.

"Believe it or not, yeah," Ezio said. "How'd things go with Tristan?"

"Uh," Milan looked at Luke and Giovanni. Neither of them said anything. "Well...we kind of had a problem."

"What kind of problem?"

"Tristan's, um...dead,"

"Dead? How?"

"The police shot him,"

"Why?"

"Gabriel was chasing him and the police blocked them off," Luke answered. "We don't know for sure what happened, but Tristan got killed." There was silence at the other end of the line. They heard a sigh before their friend spoke again.

"Did you get any information out of him?"

"A little," Giovanni replied. "He's been lying to the CIA and has worked with the Hône Order a couple times."

"Okay," Ezio scratched the back of his head as his mind raced. He couldn't figure out if Tristan's death was a good thing or not. *On one hand, we don't have to worry about him anymore, but the police will be investigating him...* "We'll talk more when we get home. Thanks, guys."

"Yeah, no problem,"

Ezio hung up and returned to the kitchen. Benito, the assassin-in-training who had thrown Milan and Giovanni into his car the previous year, was now sitting at the table, having woken up a few minutes earlier and come in for a drink. He had been startled to find so many people in there, especially when those people included Ezio and Santos. He barely recognized Ezio at first; the boy had changed quite a bit in the past nine months. He was taller, his hair was shorter, and his forehead was constantly creased with subconscious worry. He was beginning to look more like an adult.

"What do you know about Tristan Clay?" Ezio asked the assassins as he stood in the doorway. Arcadia shifted his weight, unhappy at the thought of the man who tried to kill him on Friday.

"That depends. What do you know?" Angelo asked.

"I know he was sent by Arcangelo to kill Arcadia, and that he is about to be dismissed by the CIA. I also know you used him to send false information to an NSA operative who in turn told me Sam was going to be killed. The third thing I know, which might be the most important, is that Tristan Clay was killed by the police just a few hours ago." Angelo seemed surprised, but at what part of his rant, Ezio didn't know. The old man held out his hands and smiled.

"Seems like you have it all in order,"

"No, I don't," Ezio said. "Arcangelo wants to kill you guys because you're rebels, and you're going against his plan by helping me. But last year you tested me, to prove that I was going to be a good assassin. Why would you do that if you never wanted me to join the Order?" Angelo hesitated. He knew the answer, but wasn't sure how to phrase it without people freaking out.

"Well, it's not that we don't want you to join the Order," the old man replied slowly. "We just don't want you to join Arcangelo's Order."

So Ezio's suspicion was confirmed. The day before —well, now it was two days before—as Ezio sat around the table with his friends, Milan had asked him why Angelo had done everything he had over the summer. Ezio had guessed he wanted him to become an assassin, just not in the same sense as Arcangelo. *"He probably wants me to be in the rebel group, like him."*

"I'm not going to do it," Ezio said. "In case you've been ignoring everything that I've said, I will not become an assassin, for any reason."

"Okay, okay, whatever," Angelo muttered, sounding remarkably like Marco whenever their mom yelled at him for something. "Look, you're obviously going to need to fight. You can't just sit back and wait for everything to blow over, because it's not. You have to man up and fight the Hône Order, whether you want to or not. It's a fact that you can't change. Training would help you. It would make you more prepared."

Ezio thought about it. As much as he hated the notion, Angelo was right. Formal training would be helpful, and he would be able to fight more effectively.

No, Ezio thought, arguing with himself. *Training would make you an assassin. They would win. Angelo would win.* Ezio, being the competitive athlete he was, could not let Angelo or the assassins win.

CHAPTER EIGHTEEN
THE LIAISON

CIA Agent who Attempted to Kill President of the Senate Shot by Police

Sun., April 6, 2014

VATICAN CITY—The police chased a lead Saturday night that related to the attempted murder of President of the Senate Aurelio Conti. An anonymous tip led state police to St. Peter's Square in pursuit of a man identified as Tristan Clay, an American CIA agent vacationing in Rome.

Authorities claim Clay was running towards them when they arrived at the scene. They identified themselves and told Clay to stop, but the CIA agent drew a weapon and aimed it at the officers. That is when four police officers fired at Clay, fatally wounding him. He was 33 years old.

The weapon Clay had with him was successfully identified as the one used at the Palazzo Madama shooting that occurred Friday afternoon.

Clay was stopped by a fifteen-year-old boy, who remains anonymous because of his age. The boy heroically tackled the shooter before he could fire at President Conti, and no one was injured.

Police are asking anyone with information about Clay to please call 112 immediately to help with the investigation.

Nero Lagorio smiled and went back to the RAI homepage. It was the national news company, much like CNN or the BBC. Plastered under the label of, "*Comunicato Notiziario Straordinario*," or "Breaking News," was the recently reported story about Tristan Clay. In another hour, as people got up to go to work and turned on the TV or radio, the nation would be up in arms over a CIA agent on Italian soil who attempted to kill a beloved Italian politician.

Placido Abate had retrieved the security footage from the Vatican and now, Nero was reviewing it. From what he could tell, there had been a grey-haired man running behind Tristan. Lagorio tried to zoom in and clear up the picture, but he couldn't get a good look at the mystery man's face. He would have forensics deal with it later in the morning.

But Lagorio was obsessive and selfish, so he didn't want someone else to find an important lead and get the credit. For the eighth time, Lagorio pressed the rewind button and watched the footage again. Shortly before Clay left St. Peter's Square, three people departed down one of the side roads. They were the only people, aside from the priest and the dog walker, who could have seen Tristan Clay.

Lagorio went through the two witness statements. They weren't very detailed, but the priest did mention something about three young men who had been near the obelisk around nine o'clock. According to the priest, one of the men had been wearing an orange hoodie with what appeared to be the insignia of a local school. Which one it was, the priest wasn't able to recall; he apparently had seen it on a building one afternoon not too long ago, and recognized it on the sweatshirt that night. He was able to identify one vital part of the logo, though: a sketched profile of a wolf.

"Abate!" Lagorio called. Placido scurried into his superior's office and stood straight before the desk. "How many secondary schools are in Rome?" Placido thought for a moment.

"Over a dozen, sir,"

"How many have their insignia's on the façade?"

"Private academies, mostly, sir," Placido answered. He himself had gone to a private academy, and there the school logo was engraved on either side of the front doors.

"And how many schools have a wolf as a part of their logo?" Lagorio asked as he read the priest's description of the insignia again. Placido didn't even bother to think about the question. He wasn't an expert on school logos; he didn't even remember his own school's crest.

"One," Lagorio answered for him. "The International Academy of Italy." Placido nodded as if he was about to say the same thing.

"You think a student is connected to Tristan Clay?" the younger officer asked timidly, trying not to sound too skeptical of his superior.

"They might not be connected, but they may have seen something."

"So what do we do? Talk to every student at the school on Monday?"

"No," Lagorio replied, resting his head on his fist as he thought. "Pull footage from the surrounding area. Try and find out where these boys were headed when they left. Maybe we can track them." Placido nodded and dashed out of the office, ready to work quickly and effectively.

As Abate was leaving, two men wearing long black overcoats walked in. One was about six foot three, the other was around five foot nine. The taller one had brown hair with too much gel in it, and held a briefcase in one hand. He had a square jaw and a professional air about him. The shorter one had balding black hair and thin wire-frame glasses. He had a pinched, scowling face, making him seem like a very unpleasant man.

"Are you Inspector Lagorio?" the taller one asked.

"*Chief* Inspector Lagorio," Nero replied with a smile.

"Agents Cardinal and Feldman, CIA," the one who had spoken before said as he and his partner quickly flashed their badges in one synchronized, fluid motion. "We're here to collect the body of Agent Clay and to help you in any way we can. Our two agencies are prepared to cooperate fully, and we hope to have this matter resolved quickly. As part of this, we have requested you share all evidence you have obtained thus far."

"I will be more than happy to share our findings, but I am afraid the body cannot be released yet as the coroner has not finished his autopsy. Does Mr. Clay have family who are asking for him?"

"No, but we will need him by the end of the week, if that's possible," Agent Cardinal replied. Feldman nodded curtly in agreement. Lagorio smiled.

"I'll be sure to have the body released as soon as possible. Now, as for evidence..."

*   *   *   *   *   *

"What's the story between Bernardo and Arcangelo?" Ezio asked Arcadia as the car bounced down the highway. Tony was driving his sons and Santos back to Rome, and Arcadia had—without warning, or permission, for that matter—jumped into the car as a sort of security detail. There was the chance Arcangelo would make a move, and Arcadia wanted to make sure that didn't happen. He wouldn't be able to prevent the assassins from doing anything, but he could certainly interfere with their plans. Tony, however, didn't want an assassin going back to Rome with them. He had hoped once they got home, this would all be over. *Wishful thinking, I suppose*, he thought as he pulled onto the A22/E45.

"Bernardo and Arcangelo are—" Arcadia stopped as a sullen look washed across his face. "*Were* half-brothers. Bernardo was older and always very sympathetic, but Arcangelo..." Arcadia paused, trying to figure out what word to use. "Arcangelo was aggressive. And that's a good trait to have when you're an assassin. One day, in 1968, Angelo asked sixteen-year-old Arcangelo if he wanted to join the Hône Order of Assassins, and the kid said yes. A few months later, Angelo was able to convince Bernardo, who was in his twenties at the time. But after a while, Bernardo saw what was happening to his younger brother, and he backed out of the Order, and tried to take Arcangelo with him. Arcangelo refused, Bernardo left, dropped off the radar, and then a year later, came back. He wanted to rejoin after his wife and kids left him. He had nothing left, and he was angry, so what better way to spend your time than killing people, right?" Ezio was quiet, choosing his next question carefully. The only sound was the steady hum coming from the engine as the car sped southward to Rome.

"Why does Arcangelo hate him so much?" he finally asked.

"Because Bernardo betrayed him. Back when Angelo was forced to step down and Arcangelo took over the Order, Bernardo threatened to expose his brother to the world. He threatened to go to the police, the government, the CIA, the NSA, the FBI, Scotland Yard—everyone. He knew just how crazy his brother was before any of us did. So Arcangelo tried to have him killed, but no one would do it since everyone liked Bernardo, and Arcangelo couldn't kill his own brother."

"Until now," Ezio muttered, remembering the old man lying on the table in a pool of blood. Arcadia nodded.

"Until now," he agreed.

Four and a half hours later, after two stops and many arguments with each other over what radio station to listen to, Tony finally pulled onto the exit for Rome. It was almost noon, and they were all exhausted from their journey. None of them had slept much—if at all—in twenty-seven hours. Ezio glanced in the rearview mirror and saw he still had a black eye; he had almost forgotten all about it. It was trivial compared to everything else that had happened. The fire, the daggers being thrown at them, Tony being held hostage, jumping out of the window...it had been more than any of them expected.

Ezio wasn't sure what he had even expected anymore. He knew, deep down, he wouldn't have killed Arcangelo. No matter what, he wouldn't have been able to do it. But he also knew Arcangelo wouldn't have just given in through diplomatic means. Arcangelo would have—had, actually—put up a fight. He wasn't going to just let Ezio walk away. And that terrified him.

He was horrified at the idea of not being able to get out of this. He was in too deep; the Hône Order would get to him eventually. At the moment, there was nothing for him to do but wait for the inevitable. Just like Angelo had said the past year.

But Ezio was determined not to allow the inevitable to happen. That fierce determination still blazed inside him; he refused to allow the Hône Order to win. But he knew sitting on his hands just waiting wouldn't get him anywhere. He knew he had to act. He just wasn't sure how.

"Do you know what Arcangelo's real name is?" Ezio asked out of curiosity. Arcadia nodded.

"Vasco Dinapoli," he replied. *Vasco*, Ezio thought. *That fits him.* The name "Vasco" meant crow, and for superstitious people, crows were a bad omen. There was no doubt Arcangelo was one of the baddest omens out there.

"What are you going to do now that you're back in Rome?" Ezio asked. The assassins would be looking for Arcadia and his nephew Matteo, as well as Angelo and Benito. Arcadia shrugged.

"Probably just make sure nothing happens to you. You know, I really think Lampedusa is your best bet..." He was still trying to sell Ezio on the whole hide-on-an-island-for-a-little-while thing. But the boy wasn't interested; going to Lampedusa would only be running away from the problem, not solving it.

"Sorry, Arcadia, but I'm not going anywhere," Ezio replied. The assassin nodded. He knew the boy meant what he said.

"I'm thinking about walking to the house Matteo's renting," the man said, changing the subject. "I'll get out when you drop Santos off."

"Are you sure?" Tony asked. "We can give you a ride."

"Not to alarm you, but there may be assassins—*bad* ones—watching your house. It'd be better if they didn't know I came back with you." Tony definitely looked alarmed, but he didn't say anything. He had decided he needed to stop freaking out about every assassin-related thing. This was their life now, and it was his fault. He was just going to have to get used to it.

CHAPTER NINETEEN
HUNTER

Capo Ispettore Lagorio briefed agents Cardinal and Feldman for hours, poring over every detail of the case. He told them everything from the events that unfolded at the Palazzo Madama to the boys that had been seen at St. Peter's Square. They walked down to the autopsy room in the basement and went over the preliminary findings with the coroner. Then, the CIA agents went to lunch around 11:45, leaving Lagorio and Abate to continue analyzing security footage.

"The one thing I don't understand," Cardinal said as he and Feldman dug into their lunches. "Is how a fifteen-year-old stopped Clay. Clay was a trained CIA agent. If he wanted to kill someone, he would have done it, regardless of some kid getting in the way." Feldman shrugged.

"I find it more believable than Clay getting shot by the police. Like you said, he was a trained CIA agent. Why would he be stupid enough to pull a gun out when there's a bunch of cops surrounding him?"

"Lagorio did say there was someone running behind Clay," Cardinal pointed out. "If we could get a facial recognition on him we might be able to figure out Clay's motives. I mean, he must have been in serious danger if he pulled out a gun when he knew he would get shot." Feldman thought about it as he ate. What Cardinal was saying made sense, but whoever was chasing Tristan Clay had to have been quite dangerous.

"Do you think it could be Hunter?" Feldman asked. Cardinal looked up, the notion sparking his interest.

"What would Hunter be doing in Italy?"

"We wondered the same thing about Oregon," Feldman replied. "Here in Italy there's no one looking for him, no one to recognize him, except for—"

"Tristan Clay," Cardinal finished, his eyes wide. "Didn't Lagorio say the man chasing Clay appeared to have grey hair?"

"Hunter started getting grey hair just a few years ago. The job got to him." Feldman said, setting his fork down. They were onto something.

Cardinal, excited at the prospect of a new lead, whipped out his cell phone and punched in a number. It rang several times before someone picked up.

"This better be an emergency, Cardinal. I'm in the middle of dinner," said a very annoyed voice on the other end.

"I need all of the files on Gabriel Hunter sent to my laptop now," Cardinal explained. "We have reason to believe he's in Rome."

The agents left money on the table and hurried back to the police station, not bothering to finish their lunches. They burst into Lagorio's office just three minutes later, out of breath and giddy with excitement.

"Has forensics gotten back to you with the picture?" Feldman asked, gripping the back of a chair to keep himself from falling over. Lagorio looked confused, but he reached into a folder and pulled out a grainy, black and white photo of the man believed to have been chasing Tristan Clay.

"You mean this?" he asked. The agents nodded and Cardinal took the photo from him.

For a moment, the two of them stared at the picture in awe. They had found him. The rogue NSA operative who had eluded four government agencies for nearly three years. But now...now they had found him. *They* had found him. Two CIA agents did what no team of operatives could in three years. They would be rewarded greatly for their work. Cardinal smiled slightly at the idea.

"Do you know him?" Lagorio asked. Cardinal and Feldman looked up at the *ispettore*.

"He's a rogue NSA operative," Feldman replied. "His name is Gabriel Hunter. We'll have a little more information for you when our superior sends it over."

"How long will that take?"

"Not very long," Cardinal said, picking his laptop up off a small table in the corner of the office. He logged on and checked the secure e-mail the CIA had all their agents use. There, waiting in his inbox, was a file labeled "Hunter." Cardinal clicked on it and set the laptop on Lagorio's desk. As Lagorio reviewed the file, Cardinal told him about the former NSA operative.

"Gabriel Hunter, thirty-six years old, went rogue after he was assigned to kill a man in his seventies. He said he refused to complete the mission because the man wasn't doing anything wrong. Hunter didn't understand that both the NSA and CIA had been chasing this guy for years, and that he had killed dozens of people, all over the world. He believed the NSA was becoming ruthless and corrupt, so he went rogue. We discovered he had been living in a small town in Oregon last year, but that was only after he left. We weren't sure where he was, until today."

"We have reason to believe that Tristan Clay recognized Hunter and was running away from him," Feldman added. "We think Clay panicked and drew his weapon when the police arrived, perhaps to shoot Hunter." Cardinal nodded.

"However, there's a slight problem," he continued. "Hunter's an expert at hiding, and there's no doubt he's already fled Rome, perhaps even the country. If we could pull all the footage from the train and bus stations, and the airports, that would be great. Maybe we could find out where he went and catch him there." Cardinal and Feldman looked at Lagorio, expecting him to say something. The detective wasn't listening, though. He was peering at the screen in disbelief.

"His final assignment was to kill Ezio Angelo Lombardi?" he asked quietly. The agents glanced at each other.

"Yes, you know who he is?"

"I know of his uncle, Ezio Renato Lombardi. He was suspected of several murders here in Italy, but was never found guilty of anything due to insufficient evidence. He was believed to be some sort of assassin."

"Angelo Lombardi was a part of the Hône Order of Assassins," Cardinal said. "He reportedly died in 2009, and ever since then the Hône Order hasn't shown up on the radar. We believe it was disbanded because of his death."

"But you can't know for sure. I mean, he could've faked his death." Lagorio muttered absentmindedly. He was working hard to try and piece together everything.

"That's a possibility, I suppose," Cardinal said, wondering what the detective was getting at.

"I think I know something," Lagorio said, the words tumbling out of his mouth before he could stop them. "The boy at the Palazzo, who stopped Clay, his name was Ezio Ferrari. When I mentioned Renato Lombardi he began acting oddly and ran off, saying he had soccer practice. I think he might be connected."

"Just because he has the same first name?" Feldman asked. "It could be a coincidence."

"What do we have to lose? Why not question him?" Cardinal asked, taking the detective's side. Lagorio suddenly made a sound and practically jumped out of his chair.

"The International Academy of Italy!" he shouted. "Why didn't I see it earlier? Abate, get me Ezio Ferrari's home address."

"*Sì, signore,*" Placido said with a quick nod of the head, and he began to type furiously at the keyboard on his desk just outside of Nero's office.

"Wait, you really think the kid has something to do with it?" Cardinal asked.

"Ezio Ferrari is a student at the International Academy of Italy. One of the boys at the Vatican was wearing an IAI sweatshirt." Lagorio replied.

"It could have been anyone! I mean, how many students go to IAI?" Feldman said skeptically.

"There are 788 students enrolled in grades K - 12. In grades 9 - 12 there are 346 students. Based on the boys' height and build in the security footage, I believe they are in high school. IAI is co-ed, and it is a fairly even ratio between the boys and the girls, with about 171 boys and 175 girls. It was raining last night, and it was cold, so the number of teenagers who would be outside during the dinner hour is most likely very low. Add in the fact they were at the Vatican—which is not exactly a hot-spot for teens—the answer is yes, I do believe Ezio is connected in some way." Feldman blinked at Lagorio. The man's logic made sense, even if it was a complex way of thinking.

"Do you think Ezio confronted Agent Clay?" Cardinal asked. Lagorio shook his head.

"He doesn't seem like one for confrontations. But I don't think this is a coincidence."

It was then that Placido rushed into the office and handed Nero a piece of paper.

"You'll never believe what I found," the young man said, his eyes gleaming with excitement. "I got Ezio's address, but even better than that, remember how I tracked the boys from last night to a residential area near the Trevi Fountain? Well, guess what? Ezio's family lives in the same residential area, at 18 Via Tiberio. And I checked on one other thing. There are three families besides the Ferraris that live in the same neighborhood, and they all have kids in Ezio's grade at the International Academy of Italy." Abate was thrilled he had done all this detective work on his own. He smiled proudly as Lagorio leapt from his chair and grabbed his coat off the coat rack behind his desk. *Maybe I'll get promoted to* ispettore *soon*, Placido thought with glee. *Especially if Lagorio gets promoted too.*

"Thank you, Abate," Lagorio said, shrugging his coat on. "Gentlemen, let's go."

CHAPTER TWENTY
18 VIA TIBERIO

An hour before Lagorio began to suspect Ezio, he, Tony, and Marco sat in the parking lot of the apartment complex, waiting for Milan to come outside. Santos had already gone up to his apartment, and Arcadia was on his way to Matteo's rental.

"So what do we tell mom about Ezio's face?" Marco asked as he changed the radio station yet again.

"We'll tell her I got hit in the face with a soccer ball," Ezio replied. "Change it back."

"No," Marco said defiantly. "And you've clearly been thinking about this."

"Would you rather tell mom the truth?"

"Not really,"

"Then that's why I've been thinking about it."

"Think she'll believe you?"

"Why wouldn't she?" Ezio asked. He had gotten hit in the face during soccer countless times. Sometimes he escaped with nothing more than a red mark, other times there would be a slight bruise. This time he ended up with a black eye.

After a few more minutes of waiting, Milan came out of the apartment building carrying his sleeping bag and backpack. Tony popped the trunk and they heard Milan tossing his stuff in. The trunk closed, and the door to Ezio's right opened.

"Long time no see," he said, climbing into the car. He glanced at Ezio's face but said nothing about it. "I see we're all still alive. That's good." Marco and Tony nodded, both remembering how close things had come to ending badly.

"Anyway, Luke, Giovanni, and I talked to Gabriel this morning," Milan said to Ezio. "He said the police will probably come after you, since you were the last person to see Tristan, so you need to come up with a story for that. We were careful enough not to show our faces to the security cameras, but I realized when I got home I was wearing my IAI hoodie—"

"They won't talk to me once they realize I wasn't at the Vatican. But if they find out you were, they'll ask you some questions. So don't lie to them, at least not about everything. If they ask about Tristan, just tell them you didn't know who he was. Tell them he asked you about the Basilica." Ezio advised. Milan stared at him.

"Dude, I know," he said, settling back in his seat. "This isn't my first time dealing with the police."

"Wait, what?" Marco interjected, spinning around as fast as his seatbelt would let him. "Did you commit any crimes?" Milan rolled his eyes.

"Of course not. I just knew some people who did, and that made me a person of interest. I didn't do anything."

"I don't know how I feel about lying to the police," their father said uneasily. Ezio looked at him in the rearview mirror.

"Seriously? What are we supposed to tell them? The truth is certainly out of the question, so I don't see any alternative."

"The police could help us," Tony said. Ezio shook his head.

"You don't get it, do you? The assassins will know if we go to the police and they'll hide."

"They could put you in witness protection—"

"Dad, *nothing* will work. We have to end this ourselves, or else it will never be over. Even if I'm in witness protection they will find a way to either make me an assassin or kill me." Ezio's voice was filled with a kind of bitterness he had never felt before. He glared in the mirror at a father who was trying to reason with his son.

"*Non capisco perché ce l'hai tanto con me, sto cercando di evitare che ci mettano tutti in prigione,*" I don't know why you're so mad at me, I'm trying to keep us out of prison, Tony said, switching to his native language. It was easier for him to argue in Italian than English.

"*La prigione sarebbe il minore dei tuoi problemi,*" Prison should be the least of your worries, Ezio spat as fluently as his father. He had been raised to be bilingual. "*Abbiamo cose molto più gravi di cui preoccuparci.*" We have bigger things to worry about.

"*Cosa pensavi che sarebbe successo?*" What do you expect will happen? Tony asked. "*Credi davvero che questa storia finirà bene se cerchiamo di risolverla da soli? Dobbiamo chiamare la polizia.*" Do you really think this will have a happy ending if we handle it on our own? We need the police.

"*La polizia non ci può aiutare, peggioreranno solo le cose. Ritarderà l'Ordine di azione, ma poi? Certo, io sarò ancora qui il 14 marzo, ma dopo? Non sarà certo quel cavolo di accordo che hai fatto con Angelo a fermarli e mi uccideranno. Con o senza protezione, arriveranno a me per colpa tua.*" Police intervention won't help, it'll only make things worse. It'll prolong the Order from making a move, but then what? Yeah, I'll still be here on March 14, but what about after that? They won't be restrained by the stupid deal you made with Angelo and they'll kill me. Protection or not, they'll get to me because of you.

"Oh, here we go again. I made a *mistake*, Ezio! I'm doing my best to correct it now. I was faced with a choice and I made the wrong one. It's not like you—" Tony was back to speaking in English, his entire face red, all the way from the tip of his nose to his ears.

"It wasn't a choice for you to make, dad!" Ezio shouted. "It's *my* life. How would you feel if I agreed to let Arcangelo kill you on your fiftieth birthday? Because that's pretty much what's going to happen to me. If I don't do what they want, I die. If I do become an assassin, a part of me is going to die. I will not be the same person. I will not be Ezio Ferrari, soccer player and kid. I will be Ezio Ferrari, murderer and destroyer of lives."

"For the hundredth time, I'm sorry I ever got you into this!" Tony bellowed just as he pulled up outside their house. Silence descended upon the car as both Tony and Ezio sat there seething while Marco and Milan stared awkwardly out the windows. Marco, unlike Milan, had understood the entire conversation. Milan had translated bits and pieces of it and knew from the last few moments nothing good had been said.

"Sorry won't end this," Ezio said quietly, opening the car door.

Tony didn't look up as the door slammed shut and Ezio walked to the front porch. The car was still running, and now Maya was standing in the doorway to greet them. Marco and Milan glanced at each other and slowly climbed out of the car. They smiled at their mother as if nothing was wrong and began unpacking the luggage from the trunk. Tony got out a moment later, trying his best to act normal. Ezio was nowhere to be found, and he hadn't yet explained to his mother why he had a black eye.

After the car was unpacked, Milan went upstairs to Ezio's room. He found his brother sitting at his desk, his backpack on the floor next to his chair, the book about the Hône Order laid out before him. He planned on hiding it downstairs on the coffee table under the other books already there when he got the chance. Right now he was too exhausted to do anything.

"Hey, you alright?" Milan asked quietly. Ezio glanced up.

"I don't know what to do," he said, rubbing his face tiredly. He flinched as his hand pressed on the bruise, causing a spear of pain to stab his upper cheek. He closed his eyes, waiting for the pain to subside, as he spoke: "I mean, what does someone do in this situation? Who do you go to?" Milan shook his head.

"I don't know, man," he replied. "You're a typical kid thrown into an atypical situation. A situation that's hard to get out of."

"The only way to get out of it is to kill Arcangelo," Ezio muttered. "That goes against everything I've been standing for, plus it's a crime. I couldn't kill him yesterday. I had three chances, and I didn't do it."

"No one's asking you to," Milan said, glancing over his shoulder as Marco appeared at the top of the stairs. "You're fifteen. No one's asking you to commit murder."

"But that's the only—"

"Screw that," Marco said, knowing what Ezio was going to say as he stood in the doorway next to Milan. "There's always more than one way to do something. We'll figure it out. Maybe not today, but eventually we will."

Ezio nodded, although he wasn't sure if he believed him, and Marco went into his own room, content his brother appeared to have gotten the idea. Milan hesitated, wondering if he should keep talking, but then left too. He felt bad for Ezio—he was like someone being thrown into a pack of wolves. He was fighting those wolves, trying his best not to get eaten. *Will he survive?* The thought popped into Milan's head before he could stop it. He wished it hadn't ever made itself known. It took him to a dark place. A place where Ezio was an assassin, or worse...

No, Milan chided himself. *Don't think like that. He* will *survive. He'll be okay. He has to be.*

* * * * * *

A couple hours later, Ezio woke up in his bed. He didn't remember going to sleep, or even when he had decided to take a nap. But he did know he needed sleep. He'd been awake for nearly twenty-eight hours, and on top of that, he had spent his time running around trying not to get burned to a crisp. *Yeah*, he thought. *I need sleep.*

He started to doze off again, and as he fell deeper and deeper into the dizzying abyss of sleep, he thought he heard the doorbell ring. It sounded too far away and too muffled for Ezio to tell for sure if it was real, or if he was just imagining it. He didn't care either way, really. He was too tired to care.

Just as he was on the brink of dreaming, he heard someone walk into his bedroom. Immediately, his mind burst through the fog of exhaustion and the worst possible scenario presented itself in his subconscious. *It's Arcangelo coming to kill you*, his brain warned. It was enough to wake him, and Ezio bolted upright, reaching for the dagger he had on his nightstand. He had hid it behind his alarm clock when he got home, and had put the hidden blade in the box Bernardo had given him, then put that in his desk drawer. He didn't want his mom to find them if she came in; he knew there would be no lying his way through that one.

It took a moment for Ezio to recognize who was standing next to his bed as he held a dagger aimed at their throat. Milan stared at him, his eyes bulging out of their sockets, looking quite frightened. When Ezio realized it was only him, he quickly lowered the blade and tucked it behind the clock again.

"What the hell?" Milan said, obviously in shock from almost getting his throat slit. "I thought we were cool!"

"We are," Ezio muttered, climbing out of his bed and brushing past him. "I thought you were Arcangelo."

"Well, I'm not, so I'd appreciate it if you don't try to *kill me* when I come to tell you that the police are here."

"They are?'" Ezio asked. He glanced over his shoulder at the clock and saw it was nearly two o'clock. Given what Gabriel had said to Milan, Ezio had assumed the police would have arrived at the house around twelve-thirty or one. But it had taken them longer to figure out Ezio was even remotely connected.

"Yeah, dad's talking to them in the living room. Mom's not home, luckily. She took Fiona to Franco's birthday party."

"Where's Camila?"

"I assume somewhere downstairs," Milan replied. Ezio nodded and walked back to the alarm clock. He took the dagger and slipped it into his sneaker, then took the box containing the hidden blade and slid it under his nightstand.

"What, are you going to stab the police?" Milan asked. Ezio shook his head.

"If they start snooping around I don't want them to find anything I can't explain."

Downstairs, Nero Lagorio had introduced himself and the CIA agents to Mr. Antonio Ferrari. Down the hall, Lagorio noticed, were two children sitting at the kitchen counter, watching the scene unfold. One of them was high-school aged, and the other seemed to be no more than ten or eleven.

"How many children do you have, Mr. Ferrari?" Lagorio asked casually.

"Five," Tony responded without hesitation. "Three sons and two daughters."

"Are they all home?"

"My sons are. One of my daughters is at a birthday party right now."

"Where is Mrs. Ferrari?"

"She took our daughter to the party. Do you mind telling me what this is about?" Tony glanced up as Ezio and Milan came down the stairs. Ezio looked tired, and the black eye seemed worse than before. Lagorio smiled.

"Ah, there's our hero," he said, ignoring Tony's question. Ezio showed no emotion on his face as he stepped into the doorway of the living room.

"I already told you everything that happened at the Palazzo Madama," the teen said. He seemed annoyed the detective was there.

"This is actually about a different, but related, case," Lagorio told him. "Did you hear about what happened at St. Peter's Square last night?" Ezio shook his head.

"I'm shocked," the detective commented, his gaze leaving Ezio to look at several picture frames hanging up on the wall. In most of them, there were only four children. But in more recent photos, there was a fifth: the boy who was standing next to Ezio. "It's all over the news. Everyone's talking about it."

"I haven't been following the news lately," Ezio replied bluntly, following Lagorio's gaze to a picture of him with his two brothers. It had been taken back in January, at Camila's birthday party, and of course Milan was wearing his orange IAI hoodie. *At least now Lagorio knows it wasn't me*, Ezio thought.

"Where were you last night between nine and nine-thirty?" the detective asked abruptly.

"Out of town," Ezio said honestly. Lagorio seemed interested at that answer.

"Where did you go?"

"Bard," Bard was the town directly next to Hône, and Ezio was sure they had driven on some road that could be considered part of the small township. It wasn't a total lie, but it was a statement that made Tony look up at his son as if he was crazy. Agent

Cardinal noticed the look he gave him, and made a mental note about Tony's agitation.

"Why were you there?"

"We went skiing," Ezio lied. He didn't know how to ski; he had never bothered to learn, despite having lived in a city that got pummeled with snow every year before moving to Rome.

"Do you have anyone or anything to prove that?" Lagorio asked. "Maybe a hotel receptionist, or a ticket?"

"We didn't stay overnight and we threw the tickets out. We didn't think we'd be interrogated by the police, you know?" Ezio said, a little bit of sarcasm coating his words. "But you can ask my dad, or Marco. They were with me."

"Marco? Is that you?" Lagorio asked, nodding at Milan. Milan shook his head.

"I'm Milan," he said. "Milan Vasquez."

"A friend of Ezio's?" The boy shook his head again.

"Foster brother,"

"Oh, how nice," Lagorio said with yet another smile. Ezio hated his smiles. They were mocking and fake. Something was off about Lagorio. Ezio had sensed it back at the Palazzo; something made him not trust the detective. He couldn't figure out what it was, though. *Maybe it's his attitude,* Ezio thought as Lagorio walked to the other side of the living room, where there was a table covered with picture frames.

"Milan," he continued absentmindedly as he picked up one frame containing a photograph of the Ferrari kids on Ezio's fifteenth birthday less than a month earlier. "That's a city here in Italy. Any connection to it?" In the photo, the kids sat around the dining room table, a chocolate cake placed in the middle, smiles on all of their faces. Looking at the picture, Lagorio decided both Marco and Milan could fit the descriptions of the boys seen at the Vatican. He just had to figure out which one it was. Perhaps it was both of them.

"No," Milan replied, sighing through his nose. He was sick of the reference. It was the only reason he didn't like his name. Nearly everyone he met made some comment about the century old city in northern Italy. "My mom just thought it was a cool name."

"I see," the detective said, setting the frame down carefully. "Did you go with Ezio to Bard?"

"No, I stayed home," Milan said, implying he had stayed at the house but really meaning 'home' as in Rome.

"What did you do last night?"

"I went to the Vatican with some friends," he answered, sticking to honesty for now. "We were working on a school project." The honesty had not lasted as long as Milan thought it was going to. *Whatever*, he thought as Lagorio nodded and glanced back at Cardinal and Feldman. Cardinal stepped forward and held up a photograph. It was a blown up picture of Tristan Clay's ID card, printed out on a piece of computer paper.

"Did you see this man at the Vatican last night?" Milan studied the picture for a moment while Ezio and Tony watched in anticipation.

"Yeah, I think I did," Milan finally responded. "He asked us about St. Peter's Basilica. He was interested in its history. Why? Who is he?" Tony glanced over at Ezio to see his reaction, since this was his idea, but Ezio still showed no emotion.

"His name is Tristan Clay. He works for the CIA," Cardinal said. He didn't think the kid needed to know the man had died. "Was he with anyone else?"

"I don't think so,"

"Was there anyone else in the square?" Milan tilted his head thoughtfully pretending to be unsure of the answer.

"Yeah, there was some other dude, but I didn't get a good look at his face."

"Did he say anything to Agent Clay?" Milan shrugged.

"Probably. I mean, he started chasing him." Cardinal and Feldman looked at each other, and Cardinal pulled out another piece of paper. He held it up for the boy to see.

"Was this the man who started chasing Agent Clay?" Milan stared at the picture in disbelief. It was a black and white photo of Gabriel that had been taken from a security camera.

"Yeah, I think so," he said quietly. He glanced over at Ezio, who only stared back at him stony-faced. If the CIA was looking for Gabriel, they couldn't know the boys were in contact with him. That would get them in more trouble than they were already in.

"Milan, we're going to need you to give us the names of your friends who were with you at the Vatican. Maybe they saw or heard something you didn't." Cardinal said kindly. He didn't suspect the boys were connected to Clay or Gabriel. They were just kids.

"Sure," Milan replied coolly, regaining his composure, pretending not to give it a second thought. "Luke Russell and Giovanni Rizzo. Luke lives at 921 Via Galvani, apartment 2C. Giovanni lives at 42 Via Blanco."

"Thank you," Cardinal said as Feldman quickly scribbled the addresses in a notepad. "I think that's it, right *Ispettore* Lagorio?"

"Yes, thank you for your help boys," Nero said, nodding to Ezio and Milan. Neither of them moved as the three officials walked into the front hall.

"Oh, and one more thing," Lagorio said, pausing by the door. He stared at Ezio, who turned and leaned back against the doorway. "What caused your black eye?" The boy looked at him with an icy gaze, something he had picked up from Marco.

"Got hit with a soccer ball," he replied. Lagorio smiled another artificial smile and ducked through the door without another word. Cardinal and Feldman glanced at each other as they quickly followed the detective. The door shut behind them, and Cardinal heard the lock slide into place. The Ferraris weren't going to let them back inside anytime soon.

CHAPTER TWENTY-ONE
UNDER PRESSURE

"What do you think?" Cardinal asked Lagorio as they sat in the parking lot of 921 Via Galvani. They were staring at the apartment building, waiting for Nero to say something. He was strangely quiet, thinking hard about the case and the testimonies they had just heard.

"I think they're lying," he finally said. Feldman, who was sitting in the backseat of the car, sighed in exasperation.

"Why would they be lying?" he asked irritably. "What do they have to gain?"

"I'm not sure," Lagorio murmured. "But something doesn't feel right. I think they know more than they're letting on. They seemed...I don't know. It was almost as though they were prepared, like they *expected* us."

"They're kids!" Feldman snapped. "How could they possibly know anything? I will say that it's pretty weird Ezio's foster brother just *happened* to be at the same place as Clay, but at the same time, Milan had no idea who Clay was. Either that, or he's one hell of an actor."

"I agree," Cardinal commented. "I think it's a fluke that Milan was at the Vatican, but it's a believable one. The kid was working on a project, and I bet on my life that if we go up to Luke Russell's apartment, he'll have the same story."

"Because they're *prepared*!" Lagorio exclaimed, frustrated these trained, government agents could not see what he was getting at. "I do not believe in coincidences. I think the boys went to St. Peter's Square to...well I don't know *what* they did, but they did something. Something that has to do with Clay."

"If they did," Cardinal said stoically, trying to keep some sort of peace between them. "I think they'd be a little more nervous while being interrogated."

"That's what I mean. They were *too* calm. Especially Ezio. It was like he was mad we were there. Like we were a predictable inconvenience or something."

"Maybe he *was* angry," Feldman suggested. "Who knows, he could have been playing video games and we interrupted his winning streak. You have to remember, *Ispettore*, he's a teenager. They're kind of a moody species." Lagorio shook his head.

"I think they know something," he muttered. He put the key in the ignition and started the car.

"What are you doing?" Agent Cardinal asked. "Aren't we going to talk to the Russell kid?"

"You said it yourself, he won't tell us anything different," the detective replied confidently. "We will probably find more, better, evidence at the station."

*   *   *   *   *   *

Back at the Ferrari home, Ezio, Milan, and Marco were standing in front of the TV, the remote in Marco's hand. He quickly put one of the news channels on and they watched as a banner with the words *"Comunicato Notiziario Straordinario"* appeared on the screen. Below the banner was the headline, *"La CIA ha tentato di uccidere Aurelio Conti?"*

"What's that say?" Milan asked.

"'Did the CIA attempt to kill Aurelio Conti?'" Ezio translated. He and Marco listened as the reporter explained the story:

"—Le autorità che indagano sul caso riportano che l'agente Tristan Clay, rappresentante della CIA americana per l'Italia, era in vacanza a Roma quando venerdì è entrato a Palazzo Madama e si è avvicinato al Presidente del Senato Aurelio Conti. Ha estratto la pistola puntandola verso il Senatore Conti ed è stato proprio allora che un giovane seduto lì vicino ha affrontato l'agente Clay. Nella collusione la pistola dell'agente Clay è caduta ed è partito un colpo. Per fortuna non ci sono stati feriti." Authorities investigating the case say that Agent Tristan Clay, the

American CIA liaison to Italy, was vacationing in Rome when he entered the Palazzo Madama and approached President of the Senate Aurelio Conti. He then pulled out a loaded pistol and aimed it at Senator Conti, and that is when a young man sitting nearby tackled Agent Clay. The gun was knocked out of Clay's hand, which caused it to accidentally discharge. Thankfully, no one was hurt.

"Nothing we don't already know," Marco, nodding happily. "That's good, right?"

"Shh," Ezio said, waving his hand as the reporter continued.

"—*La CIA nega qualsiasi coinvolgimento con l'attentato di Clay verso il Senatore Conti, ma molte persone a livello mondiale ritengono che si sia trattato di un colpo commissionato dall'agenzia americana. La polizia di stato non ha rilasciato commenti che possano indicare eventuali sospetti sul coinvolgimento della CIA, ma ha comunque divulgato una foto dell'uomo che si ritiene sia collegato a Tristan Clay. L'ex agente segreto dell'Agenzia Nazionale per la Sicurezza Gabriel Hunter è stato visto inseguire l'agente Clay in Piazza San Pietro ed è attualmente ricercato per accertamenti dalla CIA. Le autorità chiedono a chiunque abbia informazioni su Gabriel Hunter, o sulla sua reperibilità, di contattare immediatamente il 112.*" The CIA is firmly denying any connection to Clay's attempt on Senator Conti's life, but many people all over the world believe this was an assassination attempt sanctioned by the American agency. State police have not made any comments suggesting they believe the CIA is involved, however, they are releasing a photo of a man believed to be connected to Tristan Clay. Former NSA operative Gabriel Hunter was seen chasing Clay at St. Peter's Square and is now wanted for questioning by the CIA. Authorities are requesting that anyone with information about Gabriel Hunter or his whereabouts are asked to immediately call 112.

Now Marco crossed his arms, processing the report in his head. Milan glanced at them both, waiting for one of them to say something. He had heard Gabriel's name mentioned in the report, but he wasn't sure what had been said about him.

"Huh," Marco said quietly.

"I take it this isn't good?" Milan asked. Ezio shook his head as he pulled out his cell phone. He went to his recent calls and looked for the last number that called him that wasn't in his contact list. He held the device to his ear and listened as it rang over and over. He hoped the number still worked, and that Gabriel hadn't trashed his burner phone yet. He got a new one every two weeks or so, in a paranoid attempt to be as under the radar as possible. He tried to remember when he last spoke with him over the phone. Had it been two weeks already?

Ezio let it ring a few more times before hanging up. Gabriel probably got rid of the phone as soon as he found out the police had pulled surveillance videos from St. Peter's Square.

"We need to find him," Ezio said. He set his phone down on the coffee table and walked over to the closet to get his coat.

"And how are we going to do that?" Marco asked. "The guy's NSA. If he wants to disappear, he'll disappear." Even though Ezio knew Gabriel was smart and would have left the country by now, they still needed his help and had to do what they could to find him.

"Yeah, but we have to try—"

"Who's in the NSA?" a voice from the doorway said. The boys whipped around and saw Camila standing there, watching them. Ezio glanced at his brothers nervously. How much had she heard?

"Uh," Marco started to say. His eyes darted anxiously between his brothers and their sister. "No one." He had panicked and given Camila the one answer she wouldn't settle for. Ezio quickly covered for him, saying: "It's a character from a TV show. It's no one in real life, don't worry."

It was a terrible lie, and they all knew it. They knew it would not work. Camila studied her brothers, wondering what would cause them to lie so *stupidly*. She was eleven years old now and not as easy to lie to as Fiona was, who was almost seven. Camila would get to the bottom of whatever this was and find out what they were trying so hard to keep a secret.

The boys held their breath, waiting for their sister to react. After another scrutinizing look, she nodded. She didn't ask what TV show they were talking about because she knew it was a lie. But she would keep quiet, until the boys began acting suspicious again. Then she would bring it up, in the hopes to find out what was really going on.

"You know she wants to be a detective when she grows up?" Milan whispered once Camila had left. "She's not going to leave this alone. Not till she gets a real answer." Ezio didn't say anything. Their nosy sister was the least of his worries at this point. He glanced down at his cell phone, willing it to ring with the number of another burner phone. But it never did.

"I guess if Gabriel's gone that means we don't have to worry about being connected to him anymore,"

Marco said, trying to look at the bright side of their very dark situation. Ezio glanced up at him.

"Not helping," he said.

"Right," Marco nodded. They stood in silence for a few minutes, waiting for something—anything—to happen. Nothing did.

"So...what channel do you think the soccer match is on?" Milan asked, glancing at the TV. The news was still on, and the reporters were continuing coverage of the same story. Now there was a panel of analysts and government officials talking with the anchor about how the whole situation with Tristan Clay would affect US-Italian ties. Ezio guessed the relationship between America and Italy would not be affected at all. Italy wasn't closely tied to the United States. If anything, it would just cause Italians to be ticked off at the CIA for a few weeks. After a while, everything would die down and people would forget Tristan Clay ever existed.

"Check 227," Ezio replied. 227 was the channel that contained RAI Sport 1, which primarily showed soccer matches.

The match Milan was looking for was indeed on channel 227. Milan and the Ferrari's favorite soccer team, Juventus Football Club, was playing against their rival, Torino Football Club. Given Juventus' record against Torino, it was expected to be an easy win, but the rivalry would keep fans glued to their televisions.

Two minutes into the second half, with a score of Juventus 2-0 Torino, the doorbell rang. Marco, Milan, and Ezio looked at each other, all of them thinking the same thing.

"I'll get it!" Ezio shouted, scrambling off the couch and sprinting to the front hall. His brothers followed, forgetting about the game, and slid across the laminate floor of the kitchen into the foyer. Ezio quickly unlocked the front door and swung it open feverishly. But when he saw who was standing on the porch, he did little to hide the despondent look that came over his face.

"What are you doing here?" he hissed, closing the door slightly so no one else in the house could see the man standing before him.

"We have a slight situation," Angelo Lombardi replied calmly. He looked past Ezio at Marco and Milan, who were staring at him as if he was an alien. He looked at Ezio again and said, "You need to come with me."

"No way, my dad—" Angelo wasn't listening, though. He was walking to the house across from the Ferraris, which belonged to the elderly Mrs. Bassani. Mrs. Bassani was in Florence for the next nine months, and she had rented her house out to Matteo Conti. Unbeknownst to her, though, was the fact Matteo was an assassin.

Ezio glanced back at Marco and Milan. They nodded, telling him to go on and follow Angelo. He stepped hesitantly onto the porch and watched as Angelo closed the door of Mrs. Bassani's house.

It was cold and drizzling, and the grey sky seemed overtly ominous. Ezio shivered, but it wasn't from the chilly air. He had a strange feeling, almost like a premonition. *But a premonition of what?*

As he crossed the street, his feet splashing lightly in the puddles, he looked back at his brothers once more. He knew that if he didn't return to their house in a few minutes, they'd come after him. They had his back.

Ezio walked up to the front door and placed his hand on the knob. He pushed the door open with his shoulder, and it squealed noisily on its rusty hinges. He remembered he still had the dagger in his shoe from when Lagorio and the CIA paid his family a visit. Ezio hoped he wouldn't need it. But he was quickly realizing hope alone wasn't enough these days.

It was quiet in the house. None of the lights were on, and it was clear no one had turned the heater on. Ezio shut the door behind him and walked further into the house. It didn't look like anything of Mrs. Bassani's had been touched, although he couldn't be sure since he had never actually been in here before. Everything seemed copacetic, like no one had been living here at all.

"Hey," a man's voice said. Ezio jumped, and his heart skipped a beat from fright. All of his instincts told him to run back to his house and lock all the doors and windows, but instead, he started to reach for his sneaker. But when he looked up at who he thought was an assailant, he was surprised to find it wasn't a man.

A teenager, not much older than Ezio, was leaning against the wall at the end of the corridor. He had dark brown hair and even darker eyes, and was only a few inches taller than Ezio. He looked no more than seventeen or eighteen, and it occurred to Ezio that this must be Matteo Conti—Arcadia's nephew.

CHAPTER TWENTY-TWO
KILL OR BE KILLED

"I see you didn't learn much from your time in Hône," Matteo snickered, amused by Ezio's reaction. "Come on." He disappeared around the corner, expecting Ezio to follow. Ezio relaxed a little and stood up, but not before slipping the dagger out of his shoe and sliding it into his pocket. He walked to the end of the hall, which led into the kitchen, and rounded the corner cautiously. Matteo was waiting down a second hall, standing beside a lit doorway. He stared at Ezio.

"What? Come on," he urged. He ducked into the room, and Ezio started down the hall after him.

He was beginning to regret coming here. The feeling of foreboding wasn't getting any better; in fact, it was getting worse with each step he took. His fingers wrapped around the hilt of the blade. *Is this a trap?* His paranoia was shooting through the roof. *Why did I come here? Why would I trust Angelo?* Sure, he was helping Ezio, but he was still an assassin. He still wanted to train Ezio. He wanted Ezio as a part of the rebel group. *He can't be trusted,* a little voice inside his head told him.

Ezio ignored the voice as he entered the room. It wasn't a room at all, really—there was a rickety staircase leading down to the basement, and walls around it to keep you from falling off the sides. A single bare light bulb hung from the ceiling, and there was a switch in one of the walls. There wasn't any wallpaper or paint, just wood paneling that created the room-like feel. The floors were made of the same paneling, and the ceiling looked to be made of some sort of plaster. It was obvious Mrs. Bassani hadn't bothered to renovate this room along with the others.

What am I doing? Ezio thought as he stepped onto the staircase. It creaked and croaked and shook as he began his descent, and he was sure it would collapse before he reached the bottom. Twelve steps later, he miraculously made it to the concrete floor below, and he allowed himself to let out a small sigh of relief. He was still on high alert, though. He didn't know what was waiting for him at the bottom of these stairs.

Ezio turned and looked around the unfinished basement of Mrs. Bassani's home. There was no furniture, save for a chair, and there were two other bare light bulbs similar to the one above the staircase. Angelo, Arcadia, and Matteo stood around the chair that sat to the right of the stairs. It was occupied by none other than—

"Gabriel?" Ezio said, confused and a little surprised he was here. Then, he noticed he wasn't here by choice. The man who Ezio thought had fled the country was tied to the chair, and looked quite angry. "What the hell?" *Oh my God, I sound like Milan,* he thought when he heard himself say one of his foster brother's favorite phrases. *I've got to stop hanging out with him so much.*

"Why would you bring *him* here?" Arcadia asked Angelo, gesturing to Ezio. "You know the Order's watching him, right? You probably just led them right to us!"

"Probably," Angelo shrugged, as if he didn't really care. Arcadia rolled his eyes. Angelo seemed to be getting more and more sarcastic with each day.

"The better question is 'why is he tied up?'" Ezio said, pointing to Gabriel.

"Thank you!" Gabriel exclaimed. Arcadia barely glanced at the NSA operative.

"He was resisting," he replied simply.

"Resisting what?"

"Coming with us. We needed him here but he refused to get in the car."

"Because when two random guys dressed in black tell me to get in a car when I'm the most wanted man in Italy, I'm gonna do it." Gabriel said sarcastically. He was *really* ticked off.

"Well, yeah," Arcadia muttered. "That's how we do things." Gabriel looked at Ezio.

"These guys are psychos," he said. His whispery voice was gone; Ezio supposed that was what happened when he got upset.

"Untie him," the teen commanded Arcadia. He turned to Angelo next. "Was this the situation you were talking about?" The old man nodded. "Why is he even here?"

"We need all the help we can get," Angelo said with a sigh, as if he couldn't really believe he was admitting needing assistance. He was, after all, one of the greatest assassins the Hône Order had ever seen.

"We caught up to him before he could flee the country. Through the *airport*, no less."

"I'm sorry, I didn't want to get to Mexico on a fishing boat!" Gabriel mocked the old man.

"It wasn't a fishing boat," Angelo snapped. "It was a cargo ship."

"Oh, *excuse me*," Gabriel scowled as Matteo cut the rope that bound him to the chair.

"I see you guys are getting along," Ezio commented facetiously. Arcadia and Gabriel glanced at him.

"We need to talk about our next move," Arcadia said, ignoring his remark.

"I'm not killing anyone," Ezio made his feelings known apprehensively, anticipating what the assassin was going to say. Arcadia looked at Angelo in exasperation.

"Look, we're going to have to compromise here. People are going to die. That's inevitable. Everyone dies. It's a part of life. We just might have to speed up that process, you know? The important thing is that *you* don't die. This is no time for selfless heroics or diplomacy. This is kill or be killed."

"I'm not a—"

"Yeah, yeah, you're not a murderer. We get it. But there is no other way."

"There has to be,"

"Actually, you're right. There is. Lampedusa or Alaska. Your choice."

"That's not a choice—"

"God you're difficult," Arcadia muttered, cutting Ezio off. Tensions were running high in Mrs. Bassani's basement. Everyone in the room wanted the same thing for Ezio; they just had different ways of obtaining it.

"Look, Ezio," Matteo said, taking a step forward. He didn't know the boy very well, but he was a teenager just like him. He spoke the same language. If anyone was going to convince him of making the right choice in this situation, it was going to be him. "You're going to have to make a lot of tough decisions, not just in the next year, but in your entire life. Sometimes you're not going to like those decisions, but you have to make them anyway. This is one of those times. You have three choices, and as much as they suck, you've got to choose one." Ezio looked at Matteo, thinking carefully. He wasn't prepared to make a decision right now. He didn't want to commit himself to anything. So, he gave a little nod, just to let Matteo know he heard him.

By now, Gabriel was standing up, ready to leave. He hadn't listened to a word Matteo was saying. He was focused on one thing: getting out of Italy. He'd go to Mexico, then maybe Colombia. Once everything calmed down, he would return to Europe and live in Switzerland as a mountain guide. He had his whole life planned out, but then Arcadia and Angelo had to mess everything up. He would never get out of the country by plane now. Surely the police would be watching for him at the airports.

"If you'll excuse me," he began as he started toward the stairs.

"You're not going anywhere," Arcadia stopped him, blocking his path. Gabriel glowered at him.

"You can't stop me,"

"You can't get out of the country,"

"Wanna bet?" Gabriel challenged him. Arcadia took a step closer to him. Gabriel didn't back down. They stood almost nose to nose, glaring at each other. Angelo didn't seem to be paying attention; he was fiddling with a dagger he must have had hidden somewhere. Ezio and Matteo watched with bated breath as they waited for someone to make the first move.

"This is not my fight," Gabriel snarled. His eyes flickered over to Ezio as if to say, "Sorry, but I need to get out of here."

"This *is* your fight. You got into this—" Arcadia had a viable argument, but Gabriel stopped it from gaining strength.

"I only got into this to save a life. Not to cause the destruction of more."

"Get off your high horse," Arcadia growled. "You're just scared, that's it. You're scared the Hône Order will come after you if you get involved. That's why you didn't kill Angelo three years ago."

"I didn't kill him because he's old and he hadn't done anything wrong in years," Gabriel spat. "He was dormant. He'll die soon enough anyway. The Hône Order might need to speed up the process of death because you guys are all lunatics, but not the NSA."

"Thanks," Angelo muttered. Gabriel shot him a brief look but quickly resumed glaring at Arcadia.

"Back down, Arcadia," the old man advised. "Mr. Hunter won't go anywhere. He knows he won't leave until all of this is settled with Ezio." Arcadia grudgingly took a step back. Gabriel did the same, and they both looked at Ezio.

"Uh, well, thank you, I guess," he said to Gabriel. Angelo was right: they needed all the help they could get. Gabriel nodded.

"Think about it," Arcadia said to the boy. "Think about how you want to go about this."

"Alright, I will," Ezio replied. "Can I go home now? Marco and Milan are probably worried about me."

No one protested his departure. Gabriel reluctantly stayed at Mrs. Bassani's house with Matteo and Angelo, knowing he had missed his window to leave the country. Arcadia left through the back door, muttering something to himself about keeping tabs on the other Hône Order assassins. But before he did so, Arcadia gave Ezio the number for Mrs. Bassani's landline. "Call me when you make a decision," he had said. Ezio only nodded and walked out of the house.

It was still drizzling when he crossed the street, and as he neared his house, the front door flew open. Marco and Milan were standing there, and had been for the past ten minutes. They had watched Mrs. Bassani's house through the window in the front hall, looking for any sign of a struggle inside. None had made itself known, however, so the boys stayed in the front hall, fidgeting anxiously as they waited for their brother to appear.

Ezio entered the house without speaking, and motioned for Marco and Milan to follow him upstairs. They went up to his room, where no one would hear them talking. Ezio explained to them what happened at Mrs. Bassani's, and how he was still limited to three choices: kill some assassins, live in Lampedusa for a few months, or live permanently in Alaska. None of the choices were very satisfying.

"Arcadia says it's kill or be killed," Ezio told them. "And I guess..." He stopped and sighed. This was crazy. He rubbed his temple fretfully. This was giving him a headache. "I guess that's really our best option."

He glanced at his brothers. They nodded resignedly. They were willing to do whatever it took to get Ezio out of this mess, no matter what the cost. Even if that meant hurting other people, that was a small price to pay. Ezio was their brother. His life meant more than any assassin's.

It was going against everything the boys stood for, and no doubt it would be more difficult than words could describe, but there was nothing else they could do. This was it.

"Okay," Marco decided. "We've got your back." Ezio nodded.

"It's settled then," he said. "We stay and fight."

CHAPTER TWENTY-THREE
NO ONE LIKES MONDAYS

"Have a good day!" Maya Ferrari called from the car. "I'll pick you guys up at three o'clock." Camila and Fiona bounded away from the car and through a gate to the left of the school building, waving to their mother without looking back. The playground lay just beyond it, and it was the place all the elementary students at the International Academy of Italy waited before the morning bell rang.

Marco, Milan, and Ezio stepped away from the car and Maya began driving towards the exit. She dropped them off every morning, and picked most of them up later that afternoon. Some days one or two of the kids would have a sports practice and would have to be picked up later that evening, or they would walk home on their own.

"Crap, we've got that test in math today," Milan muttered as they walked up the steps of IAI. Middle and high schoolers were allowed in the building before 8:00, as long as they didn't "cause a disturbance," according to the school's rules. "Think she'll give us time to study in class?" Ezio nodded.

"She usually does,"

As they neared the doors, Ezio glanced up and saw the huge emblem carved into the concrete façade of IAI. A profile of a wolf with an arc above it, a star at one end of the arc, was engraved above the center set of doors.

Milan opened the door on the far left of the logo and ducked inside. Marco followed, holding the door for Ezio, who lagged behind. Something wasn't right. There was something in the air, and this time, it wasn't rain. It felt like someone was watching him.

The premonition he had felt the day before was creeping into him again as he looked around. The entire campus seemed grey in the gloom. Clouds hung low in the sky, threatening rain again. For a moment, everything was quiet. Calm.

"Ezio?" Marco said. His brother didn't move.

Then, when everything else was still, a single crow cawed from a nearby tree. Ezio couldn't see it, but he knew it was there. He knew what else was there. *Vasco.*

"He's here," Ezio said quietly. He scanned the road and the parking lot to the right of the school. He gazed out at the baseball field that was across the street. He glanced over at the playground.

There he was.

Ezio felt the blood rush to his head as he dropped his backpack to the ground. His heart pounded in his chest as he jumped over the rail of the platform. He landed hard on his feet, scraping his right hand as he outstretched it to keep himself from losing his balance. He leapt forward toward the tree line of the playground. Arcangelo was standing there, smiling maniacally. Only five feet away stood Fiona, holding a basketball, grinning as she prepared to shoot it at the basket. Ezio reached the tree line, ready to attack.

But then, he was gone.

Fiona watched as Ezio crashed into the bushes. He quickly scrambled to his feet as Marco rushed down the steps, choosing to take the long way instead of jumping off the landing.

Fiona stared at her brother, whose uniform was covered in dirt and leaves. Ezio looked crazed, and his black eye did not help his appearance.

"Did you see that man?" he gasped. Fiona didn't reply. She didn't know what he was talking about. She hadn't seen a man in the bushes.

"The man!" he shouted at her. "The man that was right here. Did you see him? He was old and wearing black and—"

"Ezio," Marco put his hand on his brother's shoulder. "You're—"

"He was here," he said to mostly himself. "He was here, he was right here. I swear to God he was right next to her."

"Ezio, stop, you're scaring Fi," Marco pushed Ezio away from their sister, who was more confused than scared. Camila pushed through a throng of kids who had gathered to watch the dramatic scene unfold and stood next to Fiona.

"What's going on?" she asked. This was just the kind of suspicious activity she had been waiting for.

"Nothing, he's just tired," Marco answered, steering Ezio towards the steps. "You know how goofy he gets when he's tired. Don't worry."

They left Camila and Fiona standing there, perplexed and only a little frightened. Marco pushed Ezio up the stairs and into the foyer of the high school.

"Ezio, you can't be—"

"I saw him, Marco, I swear. He was there, right next to where Fiona was playing."

"Calm down," Marco said, brushing some dirt off Ezio's school sweatshirt. "Even if he was here, nothing's going to happen to Fiona. Or Camila. School is probably the safest place to be right now."

"What if he takes them? Or kills them?" Ezio asked, his brow creased with worry as he spoke in a frantic tone, not bothering to lower his voice despite the groups of kids walking past. "He wasn't afraid to kill you, or dad. It'll be my fault if anything happens to them." Marco hesitated. Just the other day Ezio had called Arcangelo's bluff. The assassin wouldn't kill his family. That's what Ezio had said, anyway. It was evident now, though, that he didn't believe his own words.

"Nothing will happen," Marco reassured him quietly. "Trust me. How much sleep did you get last night?" Ezio thought for a second, his eyes clouding over as he tried to form a real, clear, thought.

"Couple hours maybe," he muttered. Marco patted his shoulder.

"See? I was right. You're just tired, that's all. It's making you freak out more than usual," he said, smirking at his own little joke. "Come on. We better get to class."

Ezio went through the rest of the day in a daze. Arcangelo had been at his school. He had been five feet from his kid sister. That was too close. Way too close.

When the final bell rang, Ezio dumped his books into his bag and headed down to the left wing of the building, which contained the elementary school. Students in grades K-5 were kept mostly isolated from kids in grades 6-12, but at the end of the day, the older siblings of kids in the elementary school could go pick them up.

As Ezio was walking down the stairwell, he pulled out his cell phone to call the number Arcadia had given him. It rang three times, and then someone picked up.

"Hello?" It was Arcadia.

"I've made my decision," Ezio said. "You said it's kill or be killed, right? Let's take the Order down. Tonight."

Chapter Twenty-Four
Rome at Night

Ezio stood in front of the bathroom mirror, checking to see if his injuries were healing. His black eye was getting lighter—slowly—and no longer hurt to touch. The bruise on his side he received when he jumped out of the castle window was disappearing quickly, but it was still a little sore. He had no other injuries, which he was grateful for. Things could have gone a lot worse in Hône.

For the first time, Ezio noticed how old he looked. Not elderly and wrinkled, but as if he was a few years older than just fifteen. He had hit a random growth spurt earlier in the year, and now he stood at almost six feet tall. He was still scrawny as ever, maybe more so now that he was taller. But he looked as though he had grown up more in the past few days than in the past few months. *I guess that's what happens when you almost get killed.*

Ezio left the bathroom and silently went back to his room. He tugged on a black hoodie and slipped on the hidden blade. He secured it around his wrist as tight as it would go—which was still too loose, as the brace could be pulled off easily—and hid it beneath his sleeve.

"Good luck," Marco said from the doorway. Ezio glanced up.

"Thanks," he replied. Marco and Milan were staying home to cover for Ezio in case their parents or sisters asked any questions. Ezio doubted they would; it was nearly one o'clock in the morning, and everyone else in the house was asleep except for the three boys.

"Be careful,"

"I will," Ezio said, picking his near empty backpack up off the floor and walking over to the doorway. "There's six of us going, so we should be safe."

"Keyword 'should,'" Marco muttered. "You have to be prepared for the worse. Everything that could go wrong, will go wrong." Ezio nodded. That was usually the case.

"Alright, I've got to get going," he said. "Thanks for covering for me."

"No problem," Marco said, stepping aside. "Just watch your back."

"I will,"

Ezio crept down the narrow staircase, thankful it wasn't nearly as loud as the one at Mrs. Bassani's house. He tiptoed down the hall, through the kitchen, and into the family room. He unlocked the back door, quietly opened it, and stepped into the cold night air.

Ezio shut the door as slowly and carefully as possible. He lifted the latch on the gate and pushed it gently, opening it just enough to fit through. He slipped around the corner, trotting down the alley formed by his and his neighbor's homes, and crossed the street to Mrs. Bassani's house, where he was greeted silently by Arcadia. Within thirty seconds, the misfit group was heading out the back door, slinking in the shadows of houses and alleys. They avoided street lamps, but the moon hanging high in the sky gave them enough light to navigate their way through the city. The rain had stopped just before sunset, allowing the clouds to dissipate and leave a black curtain dotted with stars in their wake. It would have been a beautiful night if the army marching with echoing footsteps had not been so preoccupied with their mission.

Angelo, Arcadia, Gabriel, Matteo, Giovanni, and Ezio were headed to the Rome headquarters of the Hône Order of Assassins. Because Ezio had attempted —but failed—to kill Arcangelo in Hône, the leader would most likely have fled to Rome, where he was safer amongst the other assassins. Therefore, the plan was simple: sneak into the headquarters and kill Arcangelo. The leader's elusiveness and cruelty was why the task required six people. That, and the fact Ezio probably wouldn't be able to kill the assassin himself.

The group stuck to the shadows, keeping their heads down. They could not afford getting caught now. Angelo couldn't because he was supposed to be dead. Arcadia and Matteo would easily be linked to Aurelio Conti, and it would be difficult to explain why relatives of the President of the Senate were hanging out with an assassin and a rogue NSA operative. Arrest was out of the question for Gabriel, not just because he was rogue, but because he was also on Italy's and America's Most Wanted lists. Giovanni and Ezio, if seen with Angelo and Gabriel, would have very difficult questions to answer. And that would not bode well for either of them.

The streets of Rome were not as deserted as they had hoped, but the assassins leading the pack knew their way around most any problem. They bobbed in and out of alleys, and the others—the ones not nearly as familiar with the back streets—did their best to keep up.

As they neared their destination, Matteo turned to talk to Ezio.

"You're sure about this?" he asked. "After tonight, there's no going back. If we succeed, the assassins might seek revenge. If we fail, well, Arcangelo will rain hell on us." Ezio glanced at Giovanni for support, but the look on his face wasn't very comforting. He took a deep breath and nodded.

"Yeah, I'm sure,"

After about twenty minutes of walking, the group finally arrived at their destination.

"What are we doing at the Palazzo Massimo?" Ezio asked as they crept toward a large, ornate building.

The Palazzo Massimo alle Terme was part of the National Museum of Rome. It housed collections of coins, jewelry, sculptures, mosaics, and frescos. It was one of four branches of the National Museum; the other three were within five and a half kilometers of the Palazzo Massimo.

The Baths of Diocletian was just down the street, with a 16th-century garden and sculptures. It had been commissioned by Emperor Maximian in 298 C.E., and was completed sometime between 305 and 306. It contained some of its original baths and rooms, which had been preserved over many years.

A little over two kilometers away was the Crypta Balbi, a large, ancient portico. Today it contained several exhibits, some of which dealt with the urbanity of Rome. Five kilometers from the Palazzo Massimo was the Palazzo Altemps, a palace that contained Greek and Roman sculptures that had belonged to noble Roman families in the 16th and 17th centuries.

"It's our way in," Matteo told him, sneaking behind Arcadia and Angelo.

"To what?"

"The headquarters,"

"It's in there?" Ezio asked loudly, shocked a place he had visited several times contained the organization trying to ruin his life. He stopped abruptly, causing Giovanni and Gabriel to bump into him.

"Shh!" the three assassins hissed at him.

"Sorry," Ezio apologized in a hushed voice. "But it's in there?"

"No, it's next door, in that building over there," Matteo explained, pointing to a four-story brick building fifteen feet away. "But the only way in is through here."

"Wait, why don't we just go through the door?" Ezio asked, pointing at a black wooden door on the front of the building. It was illuminated in orange light cast by a nearby street lamp. Matteo straightened up and craned his neck as he gazed at the entrance.

"Yeah, guys, why don't we just go through the front?" he asked Angelo and Arcadia.

"It wouldn't be half as fun," Arcadia replied as they went around the side of the Palazzo Massimo.

Angelo knelt down and pulled out a lock pick set. He began working at the lock while Arcadia and Gabriel kept watch. Ezio and Giovanni stood awkwardly next to Matteo.

"How old are you?" Giovanni asked the young assassin, trying to make small talk. He was curious; Matteo was the first, and hopefully the last, teenage assassin he had met.

"Seventeen," he answered. "I'll be eighteen in June, though."

"Did you get trained when you were sixteen?" Matteo nodded.

"I found out Arcadia was an assassin when I was thirteen, and I wanted in. I was having some issues with my dad, so I was trying to piss him off. You know how that is. Well, wouldn't you know Arcadia was in this dwindling rebel group and needed help, so when I was old enough, he recommended me to Arcangelo. I was trained, and I began working as a spy for the rebels. Everything was going well until Arcangelo started getting suspicious a few months ago."

"How'd he figure it out?" Ezio asked.

"We're not exactly sure. No one in the Order has any reason to suspect my disloyalty. Everyone knew about Angelo, and since Arcadia is Angelo's right hand man, everyone thought he'd be in on it too. But how Arcangelo found out about me, I'm not sure."

"Do you think someone sold you out?" Gabriel suggested, jumping in on the boys' conversation. Matteo pondered the idea.

"No one else knew about my involvement with the rebel group. No one but Arcadia, Angelo, Bernardo, and...hey Angelo, does Benito know you're against Arcangelo?"

"Everyone knows I'm against him," Angelo muttered.

"Does Benito know I'm in this group?" Angelo stopped picking the lock and looked up. Arcadia turned around, suddenly interested.

"That's a good question," Angelo murmured, considering the possibility that Benito had sold Matteo out.

"Where is Benito?" Arcadia asked.

"I left him at the compound," the oldest assassin replied. Then, he shook his head in remembrance. "Actually, no, I didn't. He went into town about an hour before I left for Rome...you don't think—" Arcadia cursed under his breath and began pacing back and forth, more alert than before. Angelo sighed and sat back on his haunches.

"Nothing ever goes as planned," he muttered.

"Okay, how much longer on that lock? We need to get out of the open," Arcadia said. "If Benito's working with Arcangelo, we might not have as much time as we originally thought."

"Almost done," Angelo replied, resuming where he left off with the lock.

"Thanks for pointing that out," Matteo said to Gabriel.

"No problem,"

"Alright, we're in," Angelo said, rising slowly to his feet. Even though he was in good shape for being an old man, he was still seventy-seven years old. His knees cracked as he stood, and it took a few moments for him to regain his energy.

"I'm getting too old for this," he muttered as he pulled open the metal door.

"Isn't there an alarm?" Giovanni asked. This was part of the National Museum of Rome. There had to be an elaborate security system inside.

"There is," Angelo answered. "But Arcadia disabled it earlier this afternoon."

"No one noticed?"

"Nope," Arcadia said, following Angelo into the Palazzo Massimo. "And if they did they certainly didn't do anything about it."

The door led to a modern service hall that had been constructed within the last ten years. It was made of cold, concrete floors and white walls. The group moved slowly through the hall, trying to minimize the amount of sound they made. At the end of the hallway was a stairwell.

There was a door at the top of the stairwell that led to one of the exhibits. Angelo and Arcadia strolled into the room, passing sculptures made of white marble. The rest of them followed, more cautious, afraid of being caught. There would be at least one security guard on duty tonight, most likely roaming any one of the four floors.

"How are we going to get into the other building if we're in here?" Ezio asked. Unless there was a tunnel connecting the museum to the Hône Order in the basement, he didn't see how they were going to get across the street. *It would make more sense to just go through the front door of the Order...* he thought. He didn't say anything, though; there was no arguing with the assassins. He knew that by now.

"We have our ways," Angelo replied. Matteo glanced back at Ezio and Giovanni and grinned.

"This should be interesting,"

Chapter Twenty-Five
Breaking and Entering

They were on the second floor of the museum, which was pitch black save for a few dimmed lights above the main staircase. The group moved as one, gliding silently across the floor. When they reached the staircase, Angelo stopped and held up his hand.

Above them came the sound of footsteps. They were different and uneven, meaning there was more than one person walking. Angelo motioned for the group to fall back into one of the exhibits. They did so, going into the room next to the staircase.

There were six sculptures in the room, each standing on a low platform made of mahogany. Attached to each platform was a small plastic sign that read "Non toccare," or "Do not touch."

"Hide," Angelo instructed as he stepped behind one sculpture. Arcadia and Matteo quickly snapped into action, while Gabriel, Ezio, and Giovanni just looked at each other.

Footsteps echoed on the staircase, forcing the three of them to move. Ezio and Giovanni darted over to a large rectangular object that stood in front of one wall. There was a gap between the piece and the wall just big enough for the two of them to fit. They crouched down, placing their hands against the stone box to steady themselves, not caring about the "Si prega di non toccare" sign.

The footsteps drew nearer and now the six intruders could hear the security guards talking. Ezio peered around the corner of his hiding place and saw there were two of them, each with a set of keys and a flashlight. The keys jingled as they walked, and the light from their flashlights bounced unpredictably on the hardwood floor. Ezio crawled backward, away from the edge, just as one guard flashed the light in his direction.

"Quel sarcofago mi fa venire i brividi," That sarcophagus gives me the creeps, the guard said.

"Anche a me. Specialmente quella maschera là," Me too. Especially the mask at the end there, the second guard added, gesturing to the left end of the sarcophagus with his flashlight. Ezio heard the guards walk closer to their hiding place. He closed his eyes and prayed the guards would not see him and Giovanni. *But even if they don't see us, they will probably hear us,* Ezio thought as his heart beat louder than ever before. He was sure Giovanni's was doing the same; Giovanni didn't handle high-stress situations well.

"*È la cosa più strana,*" That's the weirdest part of the whole thing, the first guard agreed. "*Non mi piace il modo in cui pare fissarti ovunque ti sposti. Dai andiamocene via da qui. Le monete del piano inferiore sono meno raccapriccianti.*" I don't like the way it stares at you no matter where you go. Come on, let's get out of here. The coins downstairs aren't as creepy.

The guards left, their footsteps growing quieter and quieter as they walked down another staircase. Ezio glanced over his shoulder at Giovanni. Even in the darkness of the exhibit, he could tell his friend was terrified.

"Think it's safe to go out yet?" he whispered. Giovanni shook his head frantically. If he had it his way, he probably would never leave their hiding place. They couldn't be absolutely sure the guards were gone—they could be waiting just outside the room, ready to ambush and arrest them. Giovanni didn't feel like getting arrested for breaking into an art museum after everything that had happened thus far.

Ezio knew it would be smarter to wait a few more minutes, but he was starting to get claustrophobic from the tight space. He inched forward on his hands and knees and poked his head around the corner. The guards were definitely gone; they were not waiting to see if anyone would crawl out from behind the sarcophagus. He peered through the darkness and saw Arcadia hiding behind the statue of Augustus as Pontifex Maximus, a sculpture of a man standing in a toga with one hand outstretched. The hand was missing, having fallen off some time ago.

The rest of the group was hiding behind other statues. Matteo was crouching behind one sculpture, and Gabriel was posing identically to another. Angelo was standing close behind one so not to be seen. Their hiding spots had worked—somehow. Ezio was glad they had been in a sculpture exhibit when the guards came by; if they had been in a room containing coins, they might have been out of luck with no good hiding spots.

Giovanni crawled out after Ezio, taking the fact he had not been tackled yet as a sign everything was safe. Ezio pulled out his cell phone and held the light emitted from the screen over the corner of the sarcophagus the guards had been talking about. There was, indeed, a creepy mask-like carving near the end.

"I think this is the Sarcophagus of Portonaccio," Giovanni said. "I saw it on a history show once."

"Who's inside?" Ezio asked.

"They don't know. Some general that looked sort of like that," Giovanni pointed to an unfinished sculpture of a man's head that sat atop the corner of the sarcophagus.

"Nice hair," Ezio muttered.

"You can look at the art tomorrow," Angelo said from the doorway of the exhibit. "Right now we need to be going."

They left the exhibit and headed back to the staircase. They went up to the third floor, then continued on to the fourth. There, they entered an exhibit filled with frescos and mosaics. The room was in a corner of the building, directly across the narrow street from the Hône Order.

"Did you cut the alarm for the windows?" Angelo asked Arcadia.

"Yes, I disabled everything in the building for twenty-four hours," he replied. Angelo, satisfied with the answer, unlocked and opened a window.

The windows of the Palazzo Massimo were large enough for a full grown man to crawl through, with ledges wide enough for one to stand on. Angelo crawled through the open window and lifted himself onto the ledge, carefully rising to his feet once outside the building.

"Are you sure you don't want me to do that?" Arcadia offered. Angelo chuckled.

"I may be old but I'm not dead," he retorted as he shot a glance at Gabriel, still a little hurt by his comment about his age the day before. He pulled on a rope tied to a flag holder. The Italian flag that was occupying the holder hung limply, as there was no wind that night.

The rope was black static kernmantle, the kind that rock climbers use. It had been tied to the flag holder months before, when the rebel group had begun planning its attack on the Hône Order. It had been a different plan than the one Angelo and Arcadia were executing with Ezio now, but it was a plan that required them to enter the building through a window nonetheless.

The other end of the rope was connected to a rod welded into the side of the headquarters. The rod seemed to have no other use, and Matteo quickly explained that he and Arcadia had put it in place there several months earlier. When Angelo pulled on the rope, he was testing to see if anyone had tampered with it. The rope did not move or fray, which meant it was as strong as ever.

"Hand me the carabiner," Angelo said, sticking his hand through the window. Matteo swung his backpack off and pulled out a small metal loop in the shape of a pear. He put it in Angelo's hand, who then reached up, clipped the carabiner around the rope, and locked it. He stuck his hand through the window again, and this time, Matteo handed him a piece of static kernmantle almost identical to the one that stretched between the museum and the Hône Order. They differed in size, as this new rope was significantly shorter. Angelo looped it through the carabiner and knotted it tightly around the sturdy metal clip. Then, he crouched down so he could see through the window, holding onto the rope with one hand.

"Okay. I'm going to go across first. I'll send the carabiner back and then start working on the other window. Wait until I'm inside before you come over."

Arcadia and Matteo nodded and watched as Angelo stood up again. He carefully turned around on the ledge so his back was against the museum. He held the rope hanging from the carabiner with both hands, took a deep breath, and pushed off the wall.

The old man went soaring through the night sky at an alarming speed, and in seconds he had hit the wall of the Hône Order legs-first. Now he was easing himself onto the ledge of the window across from them, gripping the corner of the wall with one hand and the rope with the other.

Once safely on the ledge, Angelo sent the carabiner back to the museum with a surprisingly forceful push for an elderly man. It stopped just short of the wall, so Arcadia climbed out onto the ledge to pull it closer. He held onto it tightly as he crouched down to look at the others.

"Give Ezio some of the things you have in your backpack," Arcadia advised. "The lighter the load the faster you'll go."

Matteo nodded and began digging through his backpack again. Ezio removed his backpack from his shoulders and unzipped it. Inside, he had a ski mask, a pair of gloves, two flashlights, and a folder, per the instructions he had received from Arcadia when they spoke on the phone.

Matteo removed two cans of spray paint from his backpack and handed them to Ezio. Ezio looked at him.

"Graffiti? Really?" Matteo grinned.

"It's Plan B if we can't find Arcangelo,"

"Doesn't that seem kind of...childish?" Giovanni asked.

"Not when they're the ones using children like me and Ezio," Matteo rationalized the vandalism.

"I thought you *wanted* to be an assassin," Ezio said. Matteo nodded.

"But I never wanted to kill people. That was the whole point of me joining this rebel group. To stop Arcangelo and the rest of the Hône Order from killing any more people, and to stop them from using teenagers like me."

"How many teenagers become assassins?"

"Not as many as before. But you would be one. The rebel group wants to take down the Hône Order, and in doing so, you would be free of the deal your dad made with Angelo."

"Not necessarily," Ezio said, remembering that Angelo still wanted to train him. Matteo shook his head.

"You would be. Angelo only wants to train you because you would be one more person to help us. He doesn't want you to go around killing politicians. He wants you to support us."

"So you haven't killed anybody?" Giovanni asked as Ezio thought about what Matteo said. Training would come in handy, especially if they were starting a war with the entire Hône Order.

"Nope," he replied. "I don't plan on killing anyone unless they plan on killing me. Like Arcangelo."

"Angelo got the window open," Arcadia interrupted, poking his head through the window.

"Gabriel, you come after me. Then Ezio and Giovanni. Matteo, you'll go last to make sure everyone gets across alright."

"Sounds good," Matteo said. He turned to look at Gabriel. "You cool with that?"

"Sure," the former NSA operative replied. He didn't look sure, though. The idea of zip-lining four stories up without a harness was a little intimidating.

Arcadia went across the rope with the same speed as Angelo, and as soon as he landed on the ledge, he sent the carabiner back to the others. He disappeared through the window, and Gabriel hoisted himself onto the ledge.

He got across safely, much to his relief. After Gabriel crawled through the window, Matteo looked at Ezio and Giovanni.

"Which one of you wants to go next?"

"You can go," Giovanni said to Ezio. "I still need to convince myself this is a good idea."

"I'm still convincing myself," Ezio muttered. He shrugged on his backpack and carefully pulled himself through the window. His legs shook as he slowly stood up. He was more frightened now than he had been at

Arcangelo's castle. Back then, he didn't really have time to think about what he was doing. Standing on the ledge at the museum, he realized four stories was rather high. He probably wouldn't survive if he fell.

"Push off the wall and swing your legs forward for momentum," Matteo told him. "Don't let go of the rope."

"Wasn't planning on it," Ezio mumbled. He reached up and grabbed the rope with both hands. He looked down—which was the one thing you *weren't* supposed to do—and instantly felt lightheaded. He was forty feet up, standing on a ledge that was two feet wide. He couldn't decide which was crazier: jumping out of the window at Arcangelo's castle, or going across a makeshift zip-line.

He looked up at the window across the narrow road. In reality it wasn't very far away, but to Ezio, it looked like there was a mile between him and the next ledge. He gripped the rope so tightly his knuckles turned white, and his hands began to sweat.

"I'm gonna fall," he said to himself. "I am going to fall."

"That's the spirit," Matteo muttered from inside the exhibit. "You'll be fine. Just push off, swing, and hold on."

"Sounds a lot easier when you put it like that," he replied sarcastically.

"Just hurry up," Ezio carefully put his sneaker against the National Museum of Rome. He took a deep breath and pushed off.

Ezio had never gone zip-lining before, but he understood the physics of it. Recreational zip-lining had a pulley system and harness to hold the person safely as they went across the line. But this makeshift zip-line had nothing but a carabiner and a rope. There was no harness to hold them safely in place, and instead, the force of gravity dragged them down.

Ezio felt as if he was falling as he left the ledge. Gravity wanted to pull him straight down, and this combined with flying forward high above the paved street made Ezio feel sick.

"Watch out for the wall," Gabriel said from the window as Ezio came towards him.

Ezio didn't hear him, though. He was too focused on not slipping or throwing up that he smashed into the wall with his legs and chest.

"Ow," he groaned as he swung back and forth on the line.

Gabriel reached over and grabbed the rope Ezio was holding onto and dragged it over to the window.

"Let go," he instructed. Ezio let go of the rope with one hand and held onto the frame of the window with the other. Once he was safely on the ledge, he let go of the rope all together. He turned awkwardly around on the narrow platform, keeping one hand on the wall, and sent the carabiner back across the zip-line. Then, he ducked into the room as fast as he dared.

Chapter Twenty-Six
Vandalism

"So what exactly are we doing?" Ezio asked as his eyes adjusted to the darkness of the corridor. They were on the fourth floor of the headquarters, which was dark and unsettlingly quiet.

"Shh,"

"Okay,"

Ezio glanced at Giovanni. Tensions were higher than they had been in the basement of Mrs. Bassani's house. This time, it wasn't because of Arcadia and Gabriel. This time, it was because of Arcangelo.

"Matteo," Arcadia whispered as they neared the end of a hallway. "When was the last time you were here?"

"Thursday morning," he replied. "Why?"

"Were you here Wednesday night?"

"Yeah,"

"How late?"

"Till around 10:30,"

"Who was here?"

"Costanzo, Lucilio, Raniero, and Filippo. Why?"

"Lucilio," Angelo grumbled. "He's one of Vasco's men. And I'm more than sure Filippo's joined them as well."

"You don't think they could be here, do you?" Arcadia asked. "I mean, it's one-thirty. They should be long gone, right?"

"Not if Benito's contacted them," Angelo replied, and Arcadia mumbled something spiteful under his breath before saying, "Where should we start?"

"We'll split up. I'll check the second floor. You and Gabriel go to the third floor. Matteo, you take Ezio and Giovanni to Vasco's study, find any information you can, and wait for the signal. Do you have the walkie-talkies?" Matteo quietly unzipped his backpack again and pulled out three black walkie-talkies.

"I've set them all for channel two," he told them as he passed the communication devices out to Angelo and Arcadia.

"Good. And from now on, you only speak of *him* as Vasco," Angelo directed. "If any of the younger assassins are here and you use his alias, they will recognize it and do whatever it takes to defend him."

So the rest of the Hône Order doesn't know Arcangelo's real name, Ezio thought as he followed Matteo and Giovanni down another hall. *Interesting.*

At the end of the hall was a set of tall doors made of solid, polished oak. They loomed sinisterly before them, looking grandly evil. Matteo approached the doors tentatively, as if they would fight back as he dragged one open.

The door opened with barely a creak as it swept across the carpeted floor, revealing a dark, still study. Ezio took out his flashlight and turned it on. There was no one in the room.

"Come on, don't be shy," Matteo said, stepping into the office.

There was an eerie feel in the room as the boys began their work. They were trespassing in a murderer's office. Why a murderer *had* an office, Ezio didn't know. But he had one, and they were sneaking around in it.

Matteo crouched down behind Arcangelo's desk and produced a lock-pick set from his backpack. He motioned for Ezio to join him and aim the flashlight at the lock. The young assassin set to work, turning and jimmying the lock on the bottom drawer of the desk. After several lengthy minutes, there was a click and Matteo mumbled something. He opened the drawer and began rummaging through stacks of paperwork.

"Take this," Matteo said as he pulled out a manila folder. He handed it over to Ezio, who flipped it open to read its contents.

"It's a list," Matteo explained. "Of all the people presently in the Hône Order. If you have this, you can use it as leverage. You can go to the police and they'd be able to track down everyone on this list."

"I thought the assassins would hide before the police could find them."

"They will. But none of them are as good as Vasco. The police would find them eventually."

"How good is Vasco?"

"As good as Angelo," Matteo replied. "Angelo trained him, Bernardo, Arcadia, and Benito. That's why it's bad if Benito is on Vasco's side. He's just as well trained as the rest of them."

Ezio put the list in the folder he had brought, and then looked to Matteo for direction. Matteo stared back at him.

"Now what?" Ezio asked. Matteo shrugged as he continued to explore the desk drawers.

"We wait, I guess."

"For what?"

"The signal,"

Ezio and Giovanni looked at each other. Waiting didn't sound like a good idea. Matteo wasn't being very quiet while he searched the desk, and if Arcangelo *was* in the building, or any assassin for that matter, they could get killed. They just wanted to get it over with, to find Arcangelo and kill him. Neither of them would probably do the killing; they would leave that to the professionals.

The signal came a few minutes later, as Matteo finished searching the last of the drawers in Arcangelo's desk. Arcadia's voice crackled quietly over the airwaves of the walkie talkies, letting them know it was safe to proceed down to the next floor. Ezio realized, as he followed behind Matteo and Giovanni, that Arcangelo's office was the only room, aside from a bathroom, on this floor. *He likes to be isolated,* he thought as the trio began to descend down the large velvet-covered steps.

Downstairs, in the silence of the second floor, Angelo was checking the dormitories. Every night, two assassins stayed at the headquarters to keep watch, to make sure the infamous Angelo Lombardi did not return for vengeance. The idea of watchmen had been proposed by Renato Lombardi two years before his death, and Angelo had enforced it when his uncle could not. Of course, when Angelo was in charge, the assassins were not watching for him. They were watching for any midnight investigations the police might care to execute. Angelo supposed now, since he was "dead," there were no more threats of police intervention, as he was really the only assassin they knew and cared about.

It was strange, walking the halls of the headquarters. He had spent most of his days here, when he was still the leader. He had rarely visited the castle in Hône; that was used for training and for leaders with large egos—much like the man who occupied it now. Renato had spent his last few years in Hône, when his health was declining. But as he was declining, he saw the monster that was Vasco Dinapoli, and he saw his ulterior motives. Vasco saw them too. He didn't want the old man talking, so he tried to kill him. But Bernardo Moretti had saved him, and Vasco escaped.

Bernardo took Renato to Verona, where Angelo had a secret compound. That day, Renato formed the rebel group of the Hône Order, the group of assassins who worked against Arcangelo. Renato told Angelo how to handle Vasco, and though he didn't like it, he complied. "Do what he says," the dying man had told him. "Hand the Order over to him. And when you have the power, tear him down. Show him no mercy." Less than four months later, Renato Lombardi died.

Angelo had sworn on his uncle's grave that he would get his revenge on Vasco Dinapoli. He would tear him down without mercy. He just needed the manpower. He needed Ezio.

Angelo stopped walking when he saw a portrait of *Arcangelo Della Morte* hanging on the wall before him. Anger and hatred surged through him like an electric current, pulsating deep within his bones. He pulled out a knife without thinking and threw it at the painting. It lodged in the canvas, the sound of the fabric tearing echoing throughout the corridors.

"*Pazzo,*" Angelo muttered the word for lunatic. He looked at the portrait to the right of Arcangelo. It was a painting of him, from when he had been leader of the Hône Order. *I'm a* pazzo *too,* he thought. *But at least I recognize it.*

"Don't move," a voice from behind cut through the silent air like the knife cut through the canvas. Angelo didn't flinch, though, and slowly raised his hands. He didn't recognize the voice, but he could tell it was a younger assassin.

"Turn around," the voice cracked from nerves. He was a rookie.

Angelo turned around slowly, keeping his hands raised. He saw a thin man in his twenties standing barefoot in a T-shirt and sweatpants. He held a dagger tightly in a shaking hand. He was scared.

"Oh my God," he gasped, his eyes widening. "You're Angelo Lombardi!"

"I am," Angelo said smoothly. "And you are?"

"Costanzo," the young man replied nervously. "Costanzo Landi."

"It's nice to meet you, Costanzo," Angelo said in a soft tone. He had to keep the conversation amiable so the assassin wouldn't think he was a threat and alert anyone else who might be in the building.

"What are you doing here?" Costanzo asked.

"Just visiting," he replied simply. As Costanzo considered the answer, his attention was drawn to the wall behind Angelo. He saw the knife in the portrait of *Arcangelo Della Morte*, current leader of the Hône Order. It was the man Costanzo had been trained to be loyal to.

Angelo followed Costanzo's gaze and saw the knife as well. He glanced back at the assassin, who looked petrified.

"Ah, yes," was all he could manage to get out before Costanzo took off at a dead sprint.

Angelo didn't bother chasing after him. Instead, he calmly pulled the walkie-talkie out of his back pocket and pressed the "TALK" button.

"Time to go," he said. "A certain Costanzo Landi has unfortunately made my acquaintance."

"We'll leave through the front," Arcadia said a moment later.

"We're on our way," Matteo told them. Angelo put the walkie-talkie away and headed down the stairs.

"We've got to get out of here," Matteo said to Ezio and Giovanni. The two looked at each other but didn't ask questions.

They quickly dashed through the a set of doors and ran down the stairs to the third floor. They continued on to the second floor, where they were greeted by Costanzo, who had doubled back and was just now reaching the staircase.

"Matteo?" he asked, startled that one of his friends was working with Angelo Lombardi.

"Oh, hey," Matteo said, giving a small wave. He shoved Ezio and Giovanni past Costanzo towards the final set of stairs. "Gotta go!"

He dashed past the young man who had once been his friend and followed the other two boys down the stairs. For a moment, Costanzo stood still, conflicted with himself. Was he supposed to chase after them or call Arcangelo?

He decided with the latter and quickly climbed the stairs. There was a phone at the top, which he used to dial a number. The answering machine picked up, as it always did, claiming the number belonged to a family in a house that didn't exist. Once the recording was over, Costanzo hurried to explain what happened. The rebels had been wrong in thinking that Arcangelo had fled to Rome. He was still in Hône, knowing what Angelo expected him to do. But the leader would hear the message and rush down from the mountain town. And he would be angry.

Chapter Twenty-Seven
A Search with no Seizure

"What should we do, sir?"

Arcangelo was standing in the hallway, staring at the portrait of himself. He had already seen his ransacked desk but was unaware anything had been taken. He was too infuriated to notice. He was at the point where no words could express his rage. He knew only one person dumb enough to want to mess up his desk: that pest named Matteo Conti. God, that kid was annoying. He was the epitome of the only thing wrong with the young recruitment age of the Hône Order. Add to that the fact Angelo Lombardi had gotten into the building...why was Arcangelo bothering to pay the assassins when they couldn't even keep an elderly man out?

It was Tuesday afternoon. Arcangelo had made the drive down from Hône when he received the message from Costanzo. Costanzo, worried he would be killed for not guarding the headquarters better, had fled Rome shortly after making the call. Arcangelo knew where he was—which was at his mother's cottage in Sorrento—but chose not to go after him. He didn't want to waste his time. Besides, it was Angelo he wanted dead. *The idiot,* he thought bitterly. *He thinks he can wage a war against the Order.*

Benito, the young assassin Angelo had been training in Verona, stood a good distance behind his leader while he waited for an answer in case his leader decided to lash out. He had also seen the ransacked desk, as well as the portrait, and had suggested just killing Ezio and getting all of this over with. But Arcangelo had refused.

"Call all of the assassins and have them convene here," he said slowly, his voice steady and monotonous. "Even if they are on a mission. And have someone repair the painting."

"What about the kid?" Benito asked. Arcangelo turned his head slightly.

"I have a very special plan for him," he replied. "A very, *very,* special plan."

Benito knew better than to ask what the plan was. He nodded and quickly climbed the stairs to the phone. As he began making phone calls, Arcangelo looked back at the portrait. He smiled slightly at the sight of the knife lodged in his two-dimensional neck. *What you've always wanted to do, Angelo,* he thought, *but have never been able to accomplish.*

* * * * * *

Ezio was helping Camila with her math homework when the doorbell rang. The sudden noise made him jump; his first thought was that Arcangelo had come for him. His hand instantly went for the dagger he now carried with him at all times. Most times, it was in his shoe, but when he was home, he kept it in his pocket.

Camila watched as he walked through the living room and into the front hall. He was acting strange again. In fact, he had been acting strange all week, ever since that Sunday afternoon when Marco said something about the NSA. He had not gotten much sleep these past few days, she noticed, as there were dark circles under his eyes. He seemed startled by loud or sudden noises, and he looked all around him whenever he went outside. It was almost like he thought someone was following him.

Ezio glanced through the window that looked out onto the porch before opening the door. He wasn't happy with who was standing on the other side, but it was someone he couldn't deny.

"Detective," he said gruffly, trying to act abrasive and adult-like. "What are you doing here?"

"I just wanted to pay you and your brother a visit," Nero Lagorio said with false cheerfulness. There was a younger detective standing behind him, his hands jammed into the pockets of his police jacket. He looked timid and a little frightened, with a boyish face and pale skin.

"This is *vice ispettore* Placido Abate," Lagorio introduced his assistant, noticing Ezio's gaze.

"Okay," Ezio said. He wasn't moving from the doorway. He wasn't going to let Lagorio inside.

"Do you mind if we come in?"

"Actually, yeah, I do," the teenager replied dryly. Lagorio's plastic smile wavered.

"And why is that?"

"My parents aren't home,"

It was a lie, and they both knew it. Maya's car was parked by the curb outside the house. She was in the basement, doing laundry, and if Ezio could hurry this conversation up, she would never know Lagorio had stopped by.

"Oh that's a shame. Do you mind if we come back later?"

"I do," Ezio said, starting to get annoyed. "I don't see why Milan and I need to speak with you anymore."

"Well, you see, a very *serious* crime was committed and you two are *coincidentally* our only two key witnesses..." Lagorio emphasized the words, letting

Ezio know he was suspicious and trying to intimidate him into a confession of some sort. But the teen stopped him with an ice cold death stare. Lagorio's voice trailed off as he saw the glare he was receiving. Ezio didn't like the way the detective was talking. He was indirectly accusing him.

"Are you accusing us of something?" Ezio asked bluntly. The corners of Lagorio's mouth twitched.

"Should I?" he asked. Ezio's stare didn't falter.

"No," the teen said firmly. He could hear his mother walking up the stairs. Lagorio would see her and know he was lying. "Have a good day." He began to shut the door, but Lagorio's foot shot out and stopped it.

"I'm not finished,"

"I am," Ezio said. He pushed the door harder, not caring if he injured the police officer.

Lagorio retracted his foot as the door slammed shut. But just before it did, he saw a woman who looked similar to Ezio walk past the hallway. He smiled.

"He's hiding something," he muttered to Abate.

"How do you know?" Placido asked.

"Because if he was innocent, he would not act so hostile and lie about the location of his parents."

Inside, Ezio hurried up the stairs to Milan's room. He was studying for a science test with his headphones in, and Ezio could hear the music blaring all the way from the doorway.

"Milan," he said. Milan didn't look up. He hadn't heard him, so Ezio stepped into the room and tapped his shoulder. His brother jumped, startled, and pulled his headphones out of his ears.

"You scared the crap out of me!" he exclaimed.

"Lagorio's here," Ezio said, the words falling out of his mouth faster than his mind could process them. "I told him mom wasn't here just to get him to leave but he wouldn't. He thinks we know something."

"About Gabriel?"

"About anything,"

"What do we do?"

"I'm not sure,"

"That's not helpful,"

The boys were panicking, which was the worst thing to do in their situation, but it was the only thing they knew how to do. Lagorio would be back, either in a few minutes or a few hours. And then what? Would he talk to their mother? They couldn't get her to leave the house, and they definitely couldn't ask her to lie if Lagorio asked any oddball questions. *We're screwed,*

Milan thought, resigning himself to the fact that he was going to go to jail for something, most likely obstruction of justice.

And just when they thought their situation could not get any worse, it did. The doorbell rang again, and the boys went into full panic mode.

"We're going to get arrested," Ezio blurted out, not caring if someone downstairs heard him. "They're going to find out we know Gabriel and they're going to arrest us."

"And if they don't find that out, they're going to arrest you for lying about mom not being home," Milan added, pacing back and forth. Ezio looked at him.

"Is that supposed to make me feel better?"

"Not at all,"

The boys rushed down to the front hall, tripping over one another in the narrow staircase. They were too late: their mother was already walking to the door.

"Hi!" Milan yelled at her, on the edge of hysteria. All rational thought processes had ceased to occur in his mind. She blinked at him like he was crazy, which wasn't completely unwarranted.

"Hello," she mumbled in confusion, reaching for the doorknob. Ezio swatted her hand away. Now she looked at both of them, wondering why they were acting so strange.

"I need your help," Milan said quickly, without thinking, grabbing her arm and pulling her towards the kitchen. "I, uh, I lost something. Outside."

"Milan—" their mom began to protest, but Milan was already dragging her through the back door to the patio.

Ezio opened the front door and tried to act nonchalant. This time, there was no fake smile from Lagorio. Instead, he held up a piece of paper that said, *"MANDATO DI PERQUISIZIONE."* Translated: "SEARCH WARRANT."

"Crap," Ezio muttered. He knew what that meant.

He stepped aside, letting Lagorio and Abate into the house. They didn't need to be invited inside; the warrant allowed them to do whatever they wanted at this point. *At least it's not an arrest warrant*, Ezio thought, trying to stay positive amid all the negativity.

"You say your mother's not home?" Lagorio asked as he nodded at Abate to go upstairs.

"Well, she might be now..." Ezio mumbled. "What exactly are you looking for?"

"We'll know when we find it," Lagorio replied. Ezio didn't like the sound of that.

"Did you just get that? You left like, two minutes ago." Gone was the hostility. Now he was just trying to get Lagorio to think differently of him. Maybe when he was arrested, Lagorio would remember his cooperation during the search and ask a judge to reduce his sentence.

"No, we had it," the detective replied. "I was just hoping we could have done this without the warrant."

"What's going on?" It was Camila, still sitting at the dining room table with a multiplication worksheet in front of her. The teen muttered something under his breath. He had forgotten all about her.

"Nothing. Don't worry about it." Ezio said tiredly, not bothering to come up with an explanation for her. She would definitely say something to their mother. Just hopefully not when Lagorio and Abate were still here.

Lagorio looked around the first floor of the house. He wasn't looking for anything pertaining to the case; he was looking for something that connected Ezio to Angelo Lombardi. He technically wasn't allowed to take anything that didn't have to do with the Tristan Clay investigation with the warrant that he had, but that didn't mean he couldn't *look* at other items in the house. Perhaps someone would call in an anonymous tip about something incriminating at the Ferrari house, and Lagorio would be able to get a different search warrant and open up a brand new case. A case that, if Lagorio solved, would make him one of the most praised detectives in all of Italy.

Lagorio walked into the family room and gazed around. It was a nice room, with a leather couch and leather chairs. There was a coffee table in the middle, facing the TV. On the shelf of the coffee table were some tomes, such as an atlas and books filled with artwork from various Italian and American museums that Ezio's parents had collected over the years. But there was one book, tucked sneakily beneath two of the art books, that looked different from the rest.

For one thing, it was brown, while the rest were brightly colored. The size was different, as it was thicker and stouter compared to the rest. The binding looked old and fragile, as if the book had been published many, many, decades ago.

The detective heard Abate walk into the kitchen, where Ezio was waiting, craning his neck to try and see what Lagorio was doing. He nodded to Abate, who understood the sign and casually blocked the boy's view. He began asking Ezio a series of questions, most of which had nothing to do with the case.

Lagorio quickly and quietly slipped the book out from underneath the others. He flipped it open to look at the publication page, to see what year it had been printed. But there was no publication page.

As he flipped through the volume, he realized it was no ordinary book. This was a handwritten account of exactly what he was looking for.

"The Hône Order," he breathed, excited that his hunch had been right. He continued turning the pages gently, wary of ripping them. This would become evidence soon.

As he neared the end of the book, he came across the list of names. There were dozens of names, birth, and death dates. They were all the leaders of the Hône Order of Assassins. Lagorio believed he had hit the jackpot.

But as he turned to the very last page, he was troubled by what he saw. The last five names on the list were different. Four included the middle names, and the only one that didn't had a small asterisk by "Ezio." There was Ciro, Renato, Angelo—then the name with the asterisk—and finally, Enzo. Why had the middle names been included for these four? And why did the asterisk key at the bottom say, "Honorable leader, not a descendent of Aetos I?"

But the one thing that troubled Lagorio—it was perhaps the most incriminating—was that next to the entry, "Ezio XXV - Angelo," there was his birth year of 1937. And next to that, where his death year of 2009 should have gone, was an empty space.

Angelo Lombardi was not dead.

Lagorio forgot for a moment that the next leader of the Hône Order was Ezio Enzo, who was undoubtedly Ezio Enzo Ferrari. He shut the book and quickly placed it back where it had originally been. He stood up, his hands shaking from the thrill of his new discovery, and rushed past Abate and Ezio.

"Thank you for your cooperation," he called as he hurried out the door. Abate wordlessly followed him, leaving Ezio standing dumbfounded in the kitchen. He glanced at the book he had hidden in plain sight. As far as he could tell, it hadn't been moved. *What was he doing in there?*

Ezio and Milan had a tough time explaining to their mother why a police officer had been in their house, thanks to Camila ratting them out. They managed to convince them both that there had been a misunderstanding, and that Ezio had—briefly—been a suspect since he'd tackled Tristan Clay twenty-four hours before he died. Maya seemed content with the answer, but Camila had a hard time believing it, based on how the detectives acted. They had been looking for something, not interrogating Ezio. But this time, she kept her mouth shut. She would have to do some investigating of her own.

CHAPTER TWENTY-EIGHT
AFTERMATH

Ezio hadn't let his guard down in over a week. Ever since the "attack" on the Hône Order headquarters eight days ago, he was always looking over his shoulder, peering around every corner, and watching his back. Lagorio acting all weird and serving a search warrant certainly didn't help. The stress was getting to him.

"When do you think he'll come after you?" Luke asked him one day. Ezio shrugged tiredly. He barely slept nowadays, and his mind was always so cloudy he could hardly form a clear thought.

"Angelo thinks they're going to wait," he answered. "Just to mess with my head." Luke nodded solemnly. *It's working*, he thought sadly. He and the rest of his friends had noticed how everything was impacting Ezio. It wasn't good.

Luke glanced down at the homework he was supposed to be working on. They were in study hall, which they had in the library during second period. He had attempted a couple of the questions, but found it difficult to concentrate when his best friend was kind of going crazy.

"Matteo's watching out for all of us, just in case," Giovanni told Luke, trying to make him feel a little better.

"How?" he asked, and Giovanni nodded towards the other side of the library. Matteo Conti sat at another table, pretending to read a history textbook. "He's like, Logan and Marco's age," he observed, staring at the young man who appeared no different from any of the other students in awe. "How's he an assassin?"

"He's actually a year older than them," Giovanni corrected. "He'll be eighteen in June. He joined the Order a couple years ago to help Arcadia fight against Arcangelo." Matteo was posing as a new student from the city of Genoa, and was attending senior classes. He had a fake name, Dario, and a fake transcript from a secondary school in Genoa, since he had dropped out nearly two years earlier to become an assassin.

"I see you're making friends with killers," Luke said, and Giovanni shook his head.

"He hasn't killed anybody yet,"

"Yet?" Before Giovanni could answer, Santos interrupted:

"Ezio, do you have that book with you? The one you took from Arcangelo's castle?"

"Yeah," Ezio pulled the old book from his backpack and handed it over to his friend. He had been carrying the book, the list of names taken from Arcangelo's office desk tucked in between the pages, with him as much as possible since Lagorio searched his house. He had a bad feeling that the detective wanted something to do with the book. Not only that, but Arcangelo might try to take it back or his mother or sisters could decide to look at it a bit more closely. *And that might be worse than if Lagorio were to get his hands on it.*

Santos flipped to the back of the book and began reading the names of all the Hône Order leaders. When he reached the end of the list, he looked up at Ezio.

"What would happen if you died?" he asked. Ezio glanced up.

"Excuse me?"

"Not literally 'die,' poor choice of words on my part. But what would happen if someone filled in your death year with 2014?" Ezio shook his head in bewilderment.

"Nothing, I don't think," he replied. "I would still be alive. Four numbers aren't going to end this."

"Well, I don't mean we just fill in the numbers. I'm talking about if we filled in the year, sent the book back to Arcangelo, and then you laid low for a while and pretended to be, you know, dead." Ezio looked at his other friends. They seemed interested in this idea. It had the potential to work.

"Hang on, let's get Matteo and ask him."

A moment later, Ezio returned to the table with Matteo. He sat down on the edge of a seat next to Milan, leaning forward with his hands folded. Santos explained his theory to the one person in their group who knew Arcangelo's patterns and motives the best. When he was finished, Matteo nodded his head but didn't seem sold.

"Two things: one, Arcangelo probably wouldn't fall for it, and two, in order to play dead you'd have to leave Rome," he told them. "And if you aren't prepared to do that, then there's no point."

Those were the only flaws in Santos' otherwise brilliant plan. It made Ezio feel a little defeated, but it's not like it changed anything. Someone had to die for this to end, and that someone had to be Arcangelo.

"Sorry," Matteo said softly, truly apologizing for something he had no control over. He felt just as bad as Ezio. He didn't want anyone to be in the position he was in. It was a difficult situation.

"I think we should just deal with this and end it," Milan said with a sigh. He was okay with killing assassins. He knew it was wrong, and that it would be tough to actually do, but there was no other option. "We need to stop trying to get around it."

There was silence as the friends thought it over. They had all agreed to help Ezio in any way they could, and they knew of the danger that promise entailed. People were going to get hurt, and there was no guarantee they would not be those people. It was a scary proposition, one that people their age should not have to deal with. Usually, people wouldn't risk their lives for some kid they hung out with. But Ezio was not some kid. He was their brother. Maybe not in the same sense as Milan was now his brother, but they were just as close. They had to help. They were ready to risk it all.

"So if the assassins are going to wait," Luke began slowly, going back to what Ezio had said earlier. "Should we go after them when they least expect it, or wait, too?"

"We wait," Ezio replied. "The day after my birthday, the assassins have to come out to kill me. Let them come to us."

"Yeah, but then you could *actually* die," Santos pointed out. Ezio shrugged.

"Let them kill me," he said, a little too loudly. A group of students sitting on the other side of the library glanced up at him. He ignored them. "If they kill me, it'll end this once and for all."

His friends didn't know what to say to that. Ezio was tired of dealing with the Hône Order, which was bad, since they had only just begun. But it had already drained so much from him. None of them had any words of reassurance, no advice to give. They could only offer their help when the time came to stand and fight.

"Great, what does *she* want?" Milan muttered a few moments later as the door of the library opened. The boys looked up and saw Sofia Greco strolling toward their table.

"Who is she?" Matteo asked.

"Somebody who *really* grinds Milan's gears," Luke said, laughing at his own joke. Milan glared at Luke to let him know this was not a laughing matter.

Sofia stopped at the end of the table, standing beside Luke's chair. He sat awkwardly, no longer laughing, unaware of what to say or do in the presence of someone his best friend hated so much. The last time they had spoken was at St. Peter's Square, and that conversation had only lasted briefly, when she walked away after Milan made some sarcastic comment. He couldn't remember what it was, as so much had happened since then.

"Hi guys," she said quietly. She glanced at Milan, but not with disgust. "Uh, I wanted to talk to you."

"Me?" Milan asked, genuinely shocked. He turned to Ezio. Was this some kind of joke? Maybe she lost a bet...

"Yeah, I wanted to talk to you about what happened at the Vatican."

"What happened at the Vatican?" Milan asked slowly. *Play dumb,* he told himself.

"I saw you talking to that man who died," Sofia replied. Milan stared at Luke and Giovanni, who stared back with wide, fright-filled eyes. She knew. She was going to tell the police.

"I don't know—"

"I'm not going to tell anyone," she interrupted. "My dad asked me if I saw anything, since we had been there that night. He's one of the officers working on the case. I didn't tell him anything, just that I talked to you guys for a bit and then headed to the car. He believed me."

The boys were astonished. This was Sofia Greco, the girl who hated Milan and treated his friends like crap. The girl who, in seventh grade, had ratted him out when he put superglue on the magnets of their science teacher's white board. That had resulted in five days' detention, not to mention fuel for his hatred of both Sofia and their teacher. Why was she helping them now?

"I don't know why you were talking to him," she continued. "But I do know you guys didn't do anything wrong."

"Is this blackmail?" Giovanni asked warily. He never trusted a word that came out of Sofia's mouth. She shook her head.

"It's not blackmail. I just don't want you guys getting in trouble."

"Oh, well, um...thank you, I guess," Milan stammered. He was still in shock Sofia—*Sofia*—was being *nice*.

"No problem," she said simply, giving a small, awkward smile. "Uh, see you guys later."

Sofia walked out of the library, leaving the boys to stare at each other incredulously. They weren't exactly sure what they had just witnessed. An act of kindness? From Sofia Greco?

"We must be going crazy," Luke muttered.

"I can't believe it's not blackmail," Giovanni remarked.

"I'm not going to question it," Milan said, shaking his head. "As weird as it is."

*　　　*　　　*　　　*　　　*　　　*

Three and a half hours later, Tony met a co-worker at a five-star restaurant in the EUR business district of Rome. They were having lunch with two American investors who were interested in doing business with their company, the International Fund for Agricultural Development, or IFAD.

They sat at a table near the center of the restaurant, waiting for the investors to arrive. Neither of them noticed a man sitting at a table in the back, left corner of the restaurant, near the kitchen door. He was wearing a suit as black as tar, and a black fedora with a single red feather tucked neatly in the narrow brim. He sat, watching Tony laugh at something his co-worker said. The man felt a putrid disgust rise up in him as he watched the father of Ezio Ferrari chuckle.

The investors soon arrived, and Tony and his companion got right down to business. Food was ordered, numbers were discussed, points were made, light jokes were cracked. The investors smiled as they agreed to do business with IFAD. The lunch was a success.

As the meeting came to a close, the man in the back corner of the restaurant rose from his seat. He made his way towards the exit, choosing the path that would bring him closest to Tony's chair. And as he passed, he deliberately ran into the chair, pretending to trip.

"*Scusi*," Tony apologized politely, pulling his chair in a little, thinking it had been his fault the man tripped. He glanced up at the man's face, or rather, where his face should have been. All he saw was a shadow before the man quickly turned away and disappeared through the door.

"Excuse me," Tony muttered distractedly, setting his napkin on the table and abruptly pushing his chair away from the table. His co-worker looked on, puzzled, as Tony ran out of the restaurant. He looked up, down, and across the street. It was a bright sunny day, and he should have had no problem picking out the man dressed in all black. But he saw no one.

Worried, Tony pulled out his cell phone. He glanced at the time. It was 2:15, so Ezio's lunch period would have ended a while ago and he would be in class now. But if Tony left a message, Ezio would call him back while they changed classes. He quickly dialed his son's number, trying not to panic.

After two rings, Tony hung up. He shook his head, as if to tell himself he was being irrational. He didn't want to worry Ezio and distract him from his studies. He was sure it was his imagination. He hadn't known the man. He couldn't have.

EPILOGUE

"Great practice today, guys," Coach Silva called as his team began leaving the field. "See you all tomorrow."

Like the normal teenagers they tried to convince themselves they were, Ezio and Milan waved goodbye to their friends as they began walking home. Coach Silva, a broad-shouldered, stout, man who had a face like a bulldog, but the voice of a chihuahua, watched as his striker and fullback walked past the gates of the school. He had noticed in the past few practices that they were not as energetic. Yes, they were still performing at the standards expected of two-time national champions, but typically Ezio and Milan were more outgoing and excitable at practice. They loved soccer more than they loved food, and that said a lot given they were teenaged boys.

Coach Silva had checked in with the boys' teachers, and their grades had slipped a little but not by much. He figured they were doing what all the other students were doing—slacking off just because the school year was winding down. He had no idea that Ezio barely ever slept now because he was scared assassins would kill him if he did. Or, that Milan woke up at every little noise the house made, his grip tightening around a baseball bat he had begun to keep in bed next to him. No one noticed that the boys slept each morning while in the safety of their classrooms; they carefully chose to sit in the back so their teachers could not see them dozing.

As long as they didn't fail two or more classes and performed well during games, Coach Silva was perfectly fine with his players being a little quieter and a little less laughable. They were good kids— always had been—and weren't disruptive during practices, but they did goof off. But it seemed the goofiness had subsided in recent weeks. Maybe they were growing up.

By the time Coach Silva began to pack up the equipment, Ezio and Milan had made it halfway down the road the International Academy of Italy was situated on. They spoke quietly as they walked, tired from the day's practice. They were both dehydrated, having gone through the last of their water bottles twenty minutes earlier.

During their conversation about a totally unrelated topic, both boys had thoughts about the Hône Order of Assassins. The organization was constantly in the back of their mind, preventing sleep and causing paranoia. It was May now—it had been almost a month since the attempts to kill Arcangelo—but neither of them could sleep through the night for fear of retaliation. They were scared, and totally unprepared. Milan didn't know what he would do with the baseball bat if an assassin broke into the house. He liked to think he'd hit them in the back of the head and save the day, but he was sure the reality would be he would just stand there like an idiot. He was a tough guy—he would fight anyone who crossed him—but put him up against a murderer by trade? Milan wasn't sure if he could do that. He'd be outmatched.

"Do we have a game this weekend?" Milan asked, unsure if it was this weekend or next that they had to get up early for a match.

"We've got that tournament over in Frascati on Saturday," Ezio replied as he pulled his empty water bottle out of his backpack.

"Oh, right. When do we play Capello?" The Capello International Institute of Rome was considered the International Academy of Italy's "mortal enemy." They had been rivals in sports for the past twenty years and showed no signs of making peace any time soon. All sports players took the rivalry seriously, and couldn't wait to play Capello just to beat them. It was no secret that IAI was better at every sport except rugby.

"I think they'll be at the tournament," Ezio said, tossing the plastic bottle into a recycling bin sitting on the sidewalk, left out by a homeowner, waiting for their trash to be picked up. "If they're not, then I know we're playing them on Tuesday next week." Milan said something about how Capello shouldn't even bother to show up because IAI would defeat them no matter what. But Ezio wasn't listening. He had noticed something on the corner ahead of them—three men dressed in black, sitting on a bench. They were too far away for Ezio to discern their faces, but he knew whoever they were, they were not waiting for the bus. He elbowed Milan to stop him from talking.

"See those guys up there?" Milan looked at the bench and nodded.

"Think they're...?" he asked, not wanting to say the word "assassins." Saying it might actually make it come true.

"Maybe," Ezio replied, but then, after further thought, "Probably."

"Should we cross the street?" Ezio shook his head. Milan looked startled. "But dude, there's three of them and only two of us." Ezio didn't say anything as they got closer and closer to the bench. Then suddenly, he started laughing.

"Oh my God, it's them," he said in relief. Milan squinted his eyes and saw that it *was* a group of assassins—just not the ones they had been expecting. It was only Arcadia, Matteo, and Gabriel, although he wasn't an assassin, he was just a rogue operative. Ezio felt a wave of relief crash over him. They were safe.

"What are you guys doing here?" he called as they neared the three of them. They looked over at Ezio and Milan and stood, in sync, to greet the boys.

"We need to talk to you," Arcadia said. Ezio and Milan slowed to a stop.

"What's up?"

"Angelo's gone," he announced. "Disappeared yesterday morning. We've checked everywhere, called every number of his, but we haven't been able to track him down."

"You think the Order has something to do with it?"

"No, but I don't think we can count on him anymore."

"What do you mean?" Ezio asked, the relief fading. Angelo was a vital asset to the operation to keep him out of the Hône Order. They needed him.

"I mean we can't count on him coming back. We can't depend on him anymore. It's just us now."

"How are we going to beat Arcangelo if it's just us? I mean, it's you three plus a bunch of teenagers. You really think we can do this without him?" Arcadia shrugged and glanced at Gabriel, who had his hands stuffed into his pockets and his head stooped low, facing away from any passing cars. He was still one of the most wanted men in Italy, with the news reporting on him every so often. The press coverage had definitely died down since those first couple weeks after he had been identified at the Vatican, but the search continued. Every European and willing South American country was on the look out for anybody matching Gabriel Hunter's description. There had been false tips called in from all over the world, ranging from Italy to China to Puerto Rico to Canada. But the real Gabriel hadn't been found yet; he was careful about where he showed his face. It had taken almost a week for Arcadia to convince Gabriel to leave the apartment he had rented in a low-profile neighborhood. And even then Gabriel refused to walk in the open streets. That bench he had been sitting on was the first time he'd been within eyesight of anyone other than Arcadia or Matteo. Maybe he was more paranoid than Ezio and Milan. Maybe.

"If Gabriel would stop being a big wuss we'd be all set," the assassin muttered. Gabriel uttered something Ezio's parents wouldn't allow him to repeat, then said, "How about you stop being a wise ass? I'm being hunted down by every government agency and police department in Europe. I can't risk being recognized. I'll help as much as I can but—"

"But you'll sit on the sidelines. It's okay, I get it." Arcadia said spitefully. Gabriel said yet another unrepeatable word.

"I'd love to help the kid, I really would, but he's not worth going to jail for. No offense, Ezio."

"None taken," Ezio replied. He didn't want Gabriel to go to jail for him either.

"Look, the Order hasn't made a move yet and they don't seem to be interested in acting any time soon," Matteo cut in, not wanting Arcadia and Gabriel to turn on each other. They needed to work together if they were going to keep Ezio from being initiated in the Hône Order of Assassins. And without Angelo, the odds of success diminished greatly. Without Gabriel, the odds were slim to none. Matteo continued: "How about we just chill out for a little while and deal with one thing at a time. Angelo's gone. We might as well believe he's dead because we don't know if he's coming back. In the past we would've been able to get a hold of him by now, or he would have called us. Let's just assume we have ten months to come up with a plan. That's plenty of time for the heat to come off Gabriel and for Arcadia to maybe recruit some more help. I'll watch after Ezio and his friends, maybe move back in with my dad so I can get access to a car and some money in case we do need to get out of the country fast. And before you say anything, Ezio, yes, I know you don't want to go to Lampedusa or Alaska, but it might be our only choice in a few months. The assassins aren't going to stop until you're one of them or dead. And considering you don't like those two options, we need a plan, and that plan is going to have to involve Arcadia— " he looked pointedly at Gabriel as he said this. "—and you. So the two of you need to grow up and get along. Alright?"

Matteo's rant was over, and the desired effect had been achieved. After a moment of silent fuming and thought, both the assassin and former government agent nodded. They could work together. They wouldn't like it, but they could do it.

"Matteo's right," Arcadia said with a sigh. "I'll keep an ear out for any chatter from the Order. If I hear something about Ezio, we'll deal with it then. And I agree that they don't seem to be gearing up to make a move."

"You don't think they're going to try and like, take him or kill him during the middle of the night?" Milan asked apprehensively, remembering his baseball bat at home.

"I doubt it," Arcadia replied, sounding very nonchalant about Milan's concerns. "Too much work. Break into a house with seven people in it, five of whom would put up a fight? The assassins might want Ezio to work for them but they're not desperate." Milan nodded, but the bat still wouldn't be too far out of his reach tonight.

"And Benito?" Ezio asked, remembering that on the night they broke into the National Museum of Rome, it had been discovered the young assassin was a traitor to the rebel group. No one ever did find out what happened to him.

"Forget about him," Arcadia muttered bitterly. "We'll take care of him soon enough."

At first, Ezio wondered what that meant, but then the words "kill or be killed" ran through his head. A lump rose in his throat as he was reminded of his agreement to that mantra. He was supposed to kill in order to keep himself from becoming an assassin by his next birthday, or a target thereafter. It was contradictory, but that was the only way. Ezio was still working to wrap his mind around that.

"Alright, guys, we'll be in touch," Arcadia said, ending the conversation. "Be careful."

"We will," Ezio and Milan said simultaneously, but both were wondering if any amount of carefulness could keep the assassins away.

Arcadia, Gabriel, and Matteo watched the two teenagers dressed in soccer uniforms disappear out of view as they continued down the street. They were all thinking the same thing, but only Gabriel had the heart, or lack thereof, to speak it:

"Think the assassins will get to them?" He turned his head away from the street as a minivan began to drive past them. Arcadia paused, but only for a moment.

"Most definitely," he replied. "But how, I don't know."

PREVIEW OF THE THIRD

EZIO FERRARI

NOVEL ON THE NEXT PAGE!

CHAPTER ONE
THE WEIGHT OF THE WORLD

A waitress wiped down the counter while a middle-aged man sat on a bar stool, drinking an espresso and reading a newspaper. Another man was sitting at a table set for two, watching the cars pass by outside. He seemed deep in thought, the waitress observed. She turned around and picked up an empty coffee pitcher. She heard the bell above the entrance ring just as she pushed the kitchen door open.

"*Sarò subito da voi*," I'll be with you in a minute, she said.

"*Grazie,*" a small voice said quietly.

The woman who had just walked in looked a little worried as she clutched a small purse and held her light pink coat closed. The waitress glanced at her briefly before continuing into the kitchen to refill the pitcher.

The woman looked around the diner and saw the man watching cars. She strode over the hard tiles, her short heels clicking with each step, and pulled out the chair across from him. The metal legs screeched awfully on the floor, making herself and the man at the counter cringe. The car-watcher didn't flinch.

"Were you followed?" he asked as she sat down. His eyes never left the road.

"No, and no one knows I came here," she answered bluntly, anticipating his next question. The man didn't say anything, so the woman continued apprehensively. "Why? Are you in danger? Is he here?"

"I'm perfectly safe," the man replied vaguely. His eyes flickered over to her. "For now."

"For now?"

"He's always been after me. But now he won't stop until I'm dead."

"I know that, but aren't you going to help Ezio?"

"I am helping Ezio," the man said, sitting back in his seat.

"You're crazy if you consider this help," the woman spat, as if her words were covered in poison.

"He'll be fine,"

"He would have a better chance of succeeding if you were actually in Rome." The man smiled at the woman and looked out the window again.

"You don't seem to understand the gravity of the situation,"

"I understand it perfectly well," she said, glaring at the man with an icy stare. He seemed unfazed.

"I'm in hot water with the Order. I don't want to meet the same fate as Bernardo."

"Bernardo," the woman scoffed. "At least Bernardo had half a brain! He was in Rome, watching Ezio. You're here in Verona, sitting in your stupid lawn chair watching from a safe distance!"

"My lawn chair is not stupid," he muttered, then shook his head. That wasn't the point. "I did what I could. Was it enough? Not at all—"

"If anything you made it worse," she interjected. He stared at her. He didn't like being interrupted.

"—but I have not abandoned him. It's just...nothing I can do will be enough. He's...well, to put it lightly, he's screwed." The woman pushed her chair back abruptly and stood up. Angelo Lombardi sighed and looked at his sister. He continued, giving one last hurrah to try and get her to understand: "I have faith Ezio will beat them."

"He is just a boy," she hissed angrily, although she knew it wasn't quite true. "And yet the weight of the world has been placed on his shoulders."

"Not the world," Angelo murmured, returning to gazing out the window. "Just Italy."

Maria glared at her brother one last time, then quickly departed from the diner. He watched as she walked down the street, away from the building and toward the train station. He would be heading to the station soon as well. Perhaps he would return to Rimini, or maybe he would venture into Ancona. Anywhere on the water would be nice. *I really should be in another country*, he thought as Maria disappeared into a crowd of people. But he wouldn't leave the country. His conscience—which he was surprised he still had—would not let him.

The waitress emerged from the kitchen and noticed the woman had gone. She set the coffee pitcher down on the counter and gazed out one of the windows. What had been troubling that woman? And why had she left without ordering anything? The diner wasn't exactly gourmet, but it wasn't bad.

*   *   *   *   *   *

ABOUT THE AUTHOR

Hannah Olin is a sixteen-year-old high school student from Western New York who began writing as a hobby at the age of seven. In November 2013, when she was fifteen years old, she released the first book of her four-part  *Ezio Ferrari* series, *Blood of an Assassin*.

For news and information on her upcoming works, you can follow Hannah at https://twitter.com/ HannahOlin, hannaholinblog.tumblr.com, and hannaholinbooks.com.

ABOUT THE AUTHOR

www.ingramcontent.com/pod-product-compliance
Lightning Source LLC
Chambersburg PA
CBHW061941170626
46813CB00006B/2486